And the Sky Didn't Fall

by Colleen McCarthy

Published by Guckian Ink

Dedicated to my Family

Chapter One

The sun was trying to get through the clouds as the rain eased off and dwindled to a slight drizzle. Seven year old Kate Hill was sad and bedraggled as she stood in the corner of the school yard and watched the other children play in the very wet grass, she wished she was back in her old school where the playground was cement and had netball hoops and where all of her friends would now be playing. She wished her mummy and daddy had never decided to move her to this horrible school with two rooms where each class sat in one long desk as the teacher struggled to take each of the four classes of junior infants, senior infants and first and second classes. There were only four junior infants and they didn't really take much teaching as all they seemed to do was draw on their copy books. There were six senior infants and they kept counting out loud even though Miss Conlon told them to be quiet. First class had the biggest group consisting of seven boys and one girl, while second class desk had three boys and three girls including Kate. The old school room was cold and whatever heat that came from the fire was impeded by Miss Conlon's large wooden desk. Kate was struggling with the Irish that second class seemed to know off by heart. She hadn't learned any Irish in England and thought she would never be able to catch on to the funny sounding words. She was aware that dun an doras was shut the door as her mum constantly shouted it at anyone who left the door open in their last home, but she was totally baffled by the conversation in Irish class. Miss Conlon had kindly drawn up some pictures of various objects and animals with the corresponding words in Irish beside them and Kate had to learn them as well as the regular homework in the evening.

She lifted her foot to look at the muck that was stuck to the bottom of her school shoe and thought how much easier it was for most of the children who were now running around the mucky yard in their bare feet. She didn't even want to wear shoes without socks never mind go in her bare feet. What an awful place this was, there was no swimming pool, no playground, no cinema, no comics and no ballet in the village, she wondered what everyone did here, so far no one seemed to care what she did, so long as she didn't get in their way. Miss Conlon who was known as The Mistress came out and announced that break was over. A mad rush of mucky children tore into the hallway and on into the schoolroom, nobody bothered to wipe their feet except Kate and she didn't really know where to wipe them as there was no mat so she just banged them on the floor. It was the dreaded Irish first thing and the children all took out their Irish readers while Miss Conlon went to the black board with a long pointy stick. She was rambling on about something called "mo asal beag dubh," why they were all staring at her? Cait, I'm Speaking to you, Kate your name in Irish is Cait so while we do that subject you will be called Cait and mo asal beag dubh is my small black donkey and that is what we are reading today. Kate suffered on for the rest of the class until the next subject which was History. More torture as Miss Conlon asked the class did anybody know who was in charge of the Country, nobody moved so Kate put up her hand to impart the news that King George the sixth was in charge he lives in Buckingham palace and we sing God save the King everyday before school. A long silence ensued as Miss Conlon slowly digested this unwelcome piece of information. Kate, thundered Miss Conlon at the by now bewildered Kate, we have our own Government here in Ireland, we have our own President and we certainly do not have a King and furthermore we will not be singing to God to save him. Our National anthem is The Soldiers Song. Do you understand? Kate nodded in confusion as she tried to remember all of this information. She was bursting from the long drink she had at break and she had to whisper to the girl nearest to her how do I get out to go to the toilet please. Lily Banaghan looked at her blankly and then as light dawned she said Oh you mean the lav, Put up your hand and say Bhuill cad agam dull amach? Kate looked at her in dismay, but knew she had to put up her hand or land herself in further disgrace. Miss Conlon looked at her with something akin to hatred, well she barked, will cod, stammered Kate but she couldn't remember the rest, however Miss Conlon got the message, out the door and around the back she said, Kate paid her one and only visit to the awful shed at the back of the school with the board with a hole in the middle, she didn't look down for fear of what was lurking there, and there was no toilet paper, no washbasin. Oh God what and awful, awful place this was.

Lunch time came and the usual mad rush of children to take their bottles of milk from in front of the fire where they were supposed to be warming up followed by another mad dash to the door to get out into the school yard. Lunches were devoured quickly, and the tepid milk also disappeared into hungry gullets. Kate took out her bottle of orange squash and her dainty triangles of ham sandwiches as she sat on the big log at the side of the school, she certainly wasn't going to sit in the mucky yard as most of her fellow scholars did.

Lily liked the look of the new girl; she was pretty, and Lily loved her curly blonde hair and above all her white socks and shiny shoes. She sidled over to the log and sat on the end hoping Kate would speak to her, Kate wasn't sure that speaking to anyone here was a good thing as they had laughed at her accent, they had laughed when she had proclaimed the King so she was going to tread carefully before she got into any more bother. Lily edged further over the log and thought about what she was going to do to get the new girl's attention. Suddenly the ball that the boys had been kicking into a makeshift goal went wide heading straight for Kate, Lily jumped up and caught the dirty object that was more muck than ball, go away she roared you nearly knocked Kate off the log. The boys all laughed but Kate was overwhelmed at this display of friendship and protection so she did the only thing she could think of and offered Lily the last of her ham sandwiches. It was devoured in two bites and so began a friendship that was to remain for the rest of their lives.

Mary Hill carefully looped up the curtains on the window of their new home, she was determined it was going to be a home and not just The House. George had really wanted to take this job in Ireland, but she had no mad longing to go back to the Land of her birth. George was English although he had an Irish Great grandfather somewhere back along the line he wasn't too bothered about where they lived so long as it meant promotion. He had told her of this vacancy for a production Engineer in the Irish plant some time ago and she had begged him to consider everything. It would mean uprooting seven-year-old Kate from her school and friends, George had an answer ready, Kate would soon make new friends, she was a smart little girl so the Irish language shouldn't be too big of a challenge. Ireland in the nineteen fifties was beginning to take shape, and after the years of rationing and queuing for all the necessities, running to the air raid shelter and putting up the blackouts it was going to be heaven to be going to Ireland, the land of milk, butter and bacon. Mary knew when she was beaten and she gave in with good grace but also with a feeling of trepidation. she had lived in England for well over a decade and had thought that was where they would remain for the rest of their lives. When she had left Ireland all those years ago she was so homesick for her parents and the farm that she never realised how soon she would get over it, and although she did still miss not having seen her mother and father for so long she had her husband and daughter to share her life with. She had met George almost as soon as she landed in England with her friend Molly Mc Gee. Molly went to work helping out in the kitchen of a Convent where her cousin was a nun. Mary got work in an aircraft/munition's factory in the industrial Estate around the Corner from the Convent. It was easy to get that kind of work at the factory during the war and Mary was ecstatic with her wages every Saturday, she was on piece work and was so diligent that she was made a chargehand within a few months. She had stayed in St. Bernard's convent with Molly for a week or two until she found digs with a lovely Irish woman from Co. Galway. George was one of the production engineers in the factory and Mary noticed the handsome blonde man with the neat moustache as soon as he stepped foot on the factory floor. George also spotted Mary's Curly red hair escaping from her hair net as she carefully kept her eyes on her work and her charges. He waited at the end of the day to see where she went and noted that she boarded the number thirty-seven bus to Maidenhead. George was persistent in his wooing, but Mary had so many obstacles in his way that a lesser man would have given up. For a start he was not a Catholic, he was English, he was rich compared to her, he had a car for heaven's sake, she would never be able to bring him home to the farm with it's thatched roof, no toilet, no running water, the list was never ending. George couldn't see any difficulty whatsoever, he loved Mary, Mary loved him, there was no problem, but as he got to know her better George realised that in Mary's world these were indeed unsurmountable obstacles. Let's make a list he said of all the things that are blocking me from making you my wife. Mary almost gave in at that point at the thought of being with George for ever and being his wife, but her stern Catholic upbringing held her back. Okay she said let's make a list. I am supposed to marry a good hardworking Irish Catholic boy preferably from a farming background, so that he can talk to my father about the weather, the cattle, the hay and the turf, while I am conferring with my mother on all things housekeeping like making bread, hens, gathering eggs and discussing the whiteness of my laundry. There are no facilities at the farm just an outside toilet, no running water, we bring it from a well. George listened attentively in total bewilderment. Let's get this sorted then he said , all right I'm not a good Irish Catholic boy but I'm a good English Protestant boy, I was Baptised and Christened George Allerton Hill, Mary giggled, I can talk to your father about farms, I was on a farm once and I saw a bull that I didn't like very much, Mary giggled again, I eat a lot of eggs so I could also talk to your mother, I can bring her water from the well. Mary almost collapsed at the thought of George in his spotless suit with it's natty waist coat arriving in to her mother with a bucket of water from the well as he surveyed the damage that the muck from the field had done to his fine leather shoes. We can be married tomorrow he grinned.

Married they were on a bright July day in 1942 in the Registry office at Maidenhead with Molly and George's Friend Charles Fuller as witnesses. They went to the pub afterwards for pie and mash. Rationing was still on, but the Landlord of the Buckinghamshire Arms came up trumps. They sat outside afterwards in the sun and drank Lemonade while Mary thought how very different she had imagined her wedding day would be. George's parents didn't attend as they lived in the north of England and petrol was rationed. It would have been unthinkable for Paddy and Annie Quinn to board a boat and come to England for the wedding of their youngest daughter, it might as well been in outer Mongolia. George's friend Charles had a brownie box camera and the registrar kindly took a black and white photo of the couple with Molly and Charles. The photo was developed and sent to Paddy and Annie with never a word about there being no Church, no Priest or that the groom was not a Catholic.

Chapter Two

As she hummed to herself and stood back to view the curtains, there was a knock at the door. Startled Mary went to answer it shoving her red curly hair from her face, they hadn't really met anyone here yet apart from the principal of the National school Master O' Hara and his assistant Miss Conlon. Mary opened the heavy front door to find The Parish priest Father Frank Hoey on the doorstep. Mary's heart sank, now that she was back in Ireland her Catholicism was beginning to take her back, She hadn't bothered going to Mass most Sunday's as it was George's favourite day of the week to have a lie in and read the papers, Kate had gone to a Catholic school but the religion didn't impinge on their life much. Good morning, Father Hoey's strong pulpit voice boomed in her ears, Mrs Hill I Believe, Mary stood there trying to think of what her mother would have done when the Parish Priest came to call. Of course he hardly ever called only if they were having the Station or when her long dead granny had passed away, but she did remember that the house was thrown upside down with the good tea set brought out of its place in the china cabinet together with the good teapot, chairs and floors were scrubbed while her mother practically licked the priest's shoes when he did arrive. All of these mad thoughts darted around her head as the priest stood looking at her strangely, are you all right Mrs Hill, he boomed? Mary pulled herself together and asked the priest politely if she could help him, she thought he looked at her strangely again as he said, well it would help if I could come in off the doorstep. Of course, Father, she said madly wondering would she bring him into the kitchen where it was warm or into the half curtained sitting room where he might not feel so comfortable and wouldn't stay long. She opted for the kitchen thinking that she could keep one eye on him if he decided to stay for tea which by now she knew she was going to have to offer him. She had biscuits, which she knew in mother's eyes would be akin to a mortal sin not to be giving the priest freshly baked brown bread or apple tart. Biscuits would have to do him she thought as she plugged in the kettle and invited him to sit down.

Well now, Fr. Hoey drummed his fingers on the table as he chewed a biscuit with some distaste, I didn't see you at Mass on Sunday last, I thought I'd meet you there afterwards, but maybe you went to late Mass he said looking her straight in the eye, Mary blushed and murmured she was sorry they hadn't met, I believe you have a child in the First Communion class, this was news to Mary who gulped and thought Oh my God, I am such a bad mother what sort of parent doesn't know what's going on in their child's life. Well she stammered Kate has only been in school for a few days I'm sure I will catch up when we get settled in. Is it just the one child you have Mrs Hill the Priest remarked looking at her as if the reason she was put on earth was to have at least five more, Oh my God she thought if he only knew that George was taking great care that they didn't have any more children as he felt that giving one child a good upbringing with everything they needed was better

14

than bringing six or seven children up with next to nothing. Not good Catholic thinking. I will expect you and your husband at the parents Communion meeting on Tuesday evening and I will see you at Mass on Sunday he said as he stood up to leave. Mary thanked God that George didn't come home for elevenses as he sometimes did.

Mary sat in the kitchen when the priest was gone trying to get her thoughts together on how she was going to get George to Mass or even to the Communion meeting, when the doorbell rang again. Oh no please let him not have forgotten anything she thought as she made her way back to the hall door, on the step was a woman about her own age with an apple tart in her hands. I am so sorry the woman said I'meant to be over earlier with the tart but I got held up and then I saw his nibs at the door and I went back home. By the way I am Sally Sheehan I live three doors down, over the greengrocers' shop with my husband Tom and children she said putting out her hand to Mary. Mary took her hand gratefully as well as the apple tart, thank you so much she said I thought you were the priest back again. Sally laughed, one visit a year is enough from him, don't let him intimidate you though, he's all right when you get the hang of him. Well he didn't see us at Mass on Sunday and he expects to see us next Sunday but I'm not sure what he is going to say when he realises my husband is not a Catholic. Sally laughed again as Mary ushered her into the kitchen, Sure he'll be grand once he gets over the shock. Mary couldn't believe she had divulged to Sally Sheehan whom she had only just met something that she had kept secret from her own family for years and the sky didn't fall. she plugged the kettle in once again as she asked her new friend to stay for a cup of tea. Are you settling in Sally asked as she looked around the fully fitted kitchen, isn't this lovely she said I wish I had some lovely presses like those, Well said Mary, It is quite nice and I am happy that we have running water and electricity as I know not everyone is lucky enough in this Country. Well we don't have a bathroom yet said Sally just a big tin bath that I fill with water every Saturday night to get the dirt off my lot. Tom has been talking about putting one in the small box room but sure he is a great man for the talk, How many children do you have Mary asked, four at the moment I'may have five if things go according to plan with this one Sally said patting her tummy. How lovely said Mary, thinking to herself how on earth would anyone manage five children, It didn't seem to bother Sally in the slightest. My oldest girl Angela is twelve and then there are the twins Amy and May aged ten, and Terence aged seven. Oh said Mary my little girl Kate is seven they are probably in the same class. Is Terence getting first Communion? Indeed he is, the little dote, said Sally, he is my baby at the moment and I don't know how he will feel about the new baby. When is the First Communion taking place Mary asked, it is on the tenth of June Sally answered, You will be off shopping for the white dress I suppose, there isn't much to dressing the boys as all they need is a shirt and trousers.

Mary thought back to her own first Communion day when she had felt for the first time like the most

important member of the family. Her older sister Meg
and brother Dan had been in their teens when Mary
arrived, while her brother Pat had been eight, a change
of life baby she had heard someone say to her mother.
Oh it was a change of life all right Annie Quinn
remarked as she thought of all the nappies she had
washed and dried, bottles that had to be heated over
the fire and sleepless nights and with her family almost
reared it was a bit of a shock to find herself pregnant
again at the age of forty three, but little Mary was a
quiet baby, good for sleeping and amusing herself.
Paddy was delighted with the new addition and called
her his little red-haired Mary. When she was getting her
first Communion, the dress that had been worn by Meg
had been got at by the Holy terrors of moths, so a new
dress would have to be purchased. Before this
unprecedented purchase could take place, a parcel had
arrived from Meg in America. It was addressed to Miss
Mary Quinn and even yet so many years later Mary
could feel the excitement at the arrival of the brown
package. When it was opened out spilled the most
beautiful frothy lace white dress that the townland of
Dufflin had ever seen. Stacked away in the corner of the
paper were white patent shoes with cross straps and
buckles and tucked into the shoes were dainty white
socks with frills on them and in the other corner a veil
with a diamond headband. Mary was speechless, she
burst out crying with the delight of it all. Oh Mammy
she said isn't Meg so good I will have to write a letter to
thank her. Indeed you will says Annie thinking to herself
how on earth is all this glory going to go down at First

Communion in the village church at Kilmacaden. The parish priest would be talking about girls being Holy and demure and the boys being mannerly and polite while Mary would be a vision of American decadence bursting with pride but committing a mortal sin on her special day with the wearing of all this affluent apparel. Mary had suddenly seen the look on her mother's face when first the dress and then the shoes and socks and veil had come out of the parcel, she knew her mother and the fear she had of trying to be better than the neighbours, so she ran for her dad who was shaving in the back kitchen. Daddy, Meg has sent me the most beautiful outfit for First Communion she said, come and see, she knew her father would want the best for his red-haired Mary. She was right, there was to be no argument Mary Quinn would be the best dressed child in the Church. Annie made up her mind to say an extra decade of the Rosary to keep jealous neighbourly thoughts away from her little girl's finery. It was a day to be remembered, Mary wore her finery and the sky didn't fall, Father John, if he was taken aback by the style of the Quinn child didn't blink an eye as he gave each child a Holy picture and a word or two of advice.

Mary knew that now she was back living in Ireland that she should be thinking of going to visit her aging parents in Dufflin, she hadn't seen them for almost twelve years. Travelling didn't happen during the war years unless you were a soldier going to save your country. They must be near their eighties now. Her brother Pat still lived with his parents while Dan and Meg both lived in America. Poor Pat she thought he must be coming up to his mid-thirties now with no wife and no hope of ever getting away to make a different life for himself, she shoved her thoughts on Pat away into the place in her head that she kept all her secrets in.

Sally Sheehan was still talking away and Mary realised that she had been only half listening as Sally's conversation broke into her thoughts, sure I will see you at the First Communion meeting in the school on Tuesday night so? Mary pulled herself together and thought quickly do you and your husband both go, Sally burst out laughing, are you mad in the head you wouldn't get Tom up there with a forty foot pole prodding him I will be going on my own. A sudden idea hit Sally as she looked keenly into Mary's worried face. Would you like me to call for you and we can walk up to the school together? Mary looked at her gratefully that would be wonderful, George can stay with Kate. That won't be the case said Sally laughing, Kate has to come too, but you can leave George at home if you want she said with a twinkle in her eye and so it was arranged that Sally and Terence would call for Mary and Kate at 6.30 on Tuesday evening.

George Hill was whistling as he let himself in from work, he hoped that Mary was as happy as he felt he was going to be in this beautiful Irish village, Work was good, he was getting on well with the management and work force, He knew that Kate would take some time getting used to the place, but he felt that if she made new friends she would be happy here too. The smell of dinner was coming from the kitchen as he hung up his hat on the hall stand, he also took off his jacket and hung it carefully on the stand as he made his way into the kitchen. Kate was sitting crying at the kitchen table with her pencil gripped tightly in one little fist as she rubbed her red eyes with the other, while Mary mashed the potatoes and tried to coax her along, it's not that bad when you get the hang of it she said to her little girl as George came and swung her up from the table, what can be so bad that we have tears sweetheart he said looking into her big blue eyes. It's this awful place gulped Kate as more tears flowed, I have to learn about mo asle beag dubh and a whole lot of other Irish words and there is nothing to do here, mummy says I won't be able to do my ballet classes anymore, there is no playground in the village and the school is cold and dirty. Oh and nobody likes me, they don't talk to me and they think my accent is funny. Miss Conlon told me off today and said she wasn't going to pray to God to bless the king. I hate this place daddy why did you bring me here.

George looked at Mary over Kate's head and said lets go into the front room until mummy has the dinner ready and we will sort this out, we will take things one by one he said in his methodical way and see what we can do to make you happy again. First of all I know there is no ballet but there is Irish dancing and you can learn that instead, I am sure the school can't be that dirty, it is sobbed Kate the toilet is just a hole in a board in a shed, and the school yard is worse, the boys play football there and nobody can get in the way or they will knock you down and nobody talks to me because they don't know what I'm Saying. George 's heart was breaking for his dainty fastidious little daughter. We will buy you some new wellington boots he said and then you won't get your shoes dirty, are you sure no one talks to you, well Kate admitted one girl called Lily did stand up for me today when the dirty ball was coming to hit me and I gave her one of my sandwiches. She said she loved my shoes and that she would see me at school on Monday. Well then said George we have something to look forward to. Tomorrow is Saturday and we will go and get the wellingtons and I'm sure mummy will help you with the Irish words. Let's have our dinner and we will all feel much better. Kate thought how wonderful her beloved daddy was as he carried her squealing into the kitchen to tell Mary they were ready to eat.

Sally Sheehan was also making dinner for her hungry husband and children. Tom and herself rarely got a chance to sit down together as when Tom came up from the shop to eat Sally went down and took over. They hoped to get someone to help out when things improved, but with the new baby on the way that didn't look likely for the near future. She thought about her new neighbour Mary Hill and the beautiful home she had, herself and her husband and daughter would probably be sitting down to dinner together in that lovely kitchen by now, or maybe they had a dining room Sally thought to herself as she teemed off the water from the potatoes, she had noticed that Mary had peeled the potatoes out of the corner of her eye when they were sitting in the kitchen, Sally only peeled them at Christmas when Tom's parents and her father came for Christmas dinner. There wasn't much time in the Sheehan household for fancy dinners. This evenings offering was bacon, cabbage and turnip, which little Terence hated, I'll eat some of the bacon Mammy and a potato please don't make me eat the cabbage and turnip. Sally looked at her youngest child, he was much more fastidious than his sisters and hated it when the girls teased him for playing with their dolls and dressing up clothes. She sighed as she thought of how Tom brought him to the football games up in the Parish field when Terence would rather be at home with her watching her knit. Mammy, he now spoke up as she quickly gave him his dinner minus the vegetables before Tom came up and called Terence a sissy for not eating up everything, Mammy, you know the First Communion day is coming can I get new clothes? Of course you can, my pet, said Sally we will get you new trousers and shirt, sure you will be gorgeous she said hugging her little man, Mammy, I want a white trousers he said earnestly, with the white shirt, the girls have white dresses so I want a white outfit too. Sally's heart sank, Tom would go mad if he heard this latest fantasy of Terence's. Eat up your dinner son she said and I will think about it, I have to go down to let your daddy up from the shop. Ok mammy, the little boy replied gulping his food as he wanted to be finished by the time Tom arrived.

Sally went down the stairs and into the shop that sold everything from a needle to an anchor as her husband wrapped up sugar and tea in brown paper bags for Mrs Mullen from across the road. Good day to you, Sally she shouted as Tom put the money in the till. Mrs Mullen was deaf so she shouted all the time and Sally shouted back at her Nice weather we are having she roared. No, I Don't need any leather, Sally, Mrs Mullen roared back that's all right so said Sally grinning. Go ahead up Tom your dinner is waiting, Thanks love Tom said wearily as he made to climb the stairs, his day started at seven am when the daily papers came and went on until ten pm at night as there was always someone wanting something especially at the last minute. He didn't mind the long hours but he felt that himself and Sally were somehow coming unstuck as they had so little time to themselves. He felt upset that the promise of help for the shop was put back again because of the new baby and the things they would have to get for it. He knew that Sally also worked hard with the children and their washing ironing, homework and the help that she gave him on days when he had to go to the cash and carry. He could hear the racket as he climbed the stairs, Angela was shouting at the twins to leave her doll alone. But Angela we are only minding her for you Amy cried. I don't want you minding her, go and mind your own. Now now girls he soothed as he went in the door what's all this blather about. He looked to see where his son was, but there was no sign of him. Can I not sit down to my dinner in peace he said in a sad voice? Of course you can daddy, his three girls ran to hug him as they all adored their father. Angela pulled out his chair while the twins sat either side of him. Where's Terence, Tom asked looking around the room, I think he went up to the loft, May said, to do his spellings. Terence also loved

23

his father but he was afraid of him He didn't like it when daddy tried to make him play football or when daddy told him to be a man when one of the girls knocked him down in one of the many daily fights that took place in the Sheehan household. He really wanted a white trousers for his first communion but from the look on his mother's face when he mentioned it didn't look too promising. He had seen short white trousers in Canny's Drapery shop when he was coming home from school yesterday.

Mary chewed her pen as she sat in their Sunny front room with its comfortable 3 piece suite, its little coffee table and the nice thick pale blue pile carpet. The writing bureau was situated in the alcove of the big bay window facing out on to the front lawn, she was writing the long overdue letter to her mother. She had written every couple of weeks when they lived in England about their lives there, the rationing, the long queues for bread, powdered milk and eggs and numerous other food stuffs that her mother had in abundance, what they did each day, and how much Kate was growing and other news relevant to their daily lives, but now she was back living in Ireland she was stuck for words, Dear Mam she had written at the top of the page, I hope that yourself, Dad and Pat are well, come on she chided herself get a move on or the morning will be over and George and Kate will be home. They had gone for a walk around the village and were going to buy wellington boots for Kate on the way back. Mary knew they had to go and see her parents sooner rather than later, they were dying to meet their granddaughter and of course

Mary's husband George. We will come and visit next weekend she wrote, we will come on Friday evening, stay for the night if you will have us, and leave on Saturday evening. That way she thought we won't have to be there for the Sunday morning, and the expected introduction of her husband to the Priest and neighbours after Mass. She was sure George would go to Mass if she asked him, but she wasn't going to take the chance. Kate is looking forward to meeting her granny and grandad and also her Uncle Pat, she has never been on a farm before and cannot believe that she will see chickens that lay eggs that don't have to be queued for and cows that give milk that doesn't come in a bottle, she is also looking forward to seeing your cat, we should arrive about 7.30pm, love from us all until then. Mary, George and Kate. She put the letter into an envelope and addressed it just as she heard the excited chatter of Kate coming in the back door.

Mummy look at my new boots, daddy says they are wellingtons but I am going to call them boots, she put the black rubber boots shiny and new on the floor beside the door, we got long socks to go inside them as Mrs Canny said they might leave rings on my legs if I didn't wear the long socks inside. Mary remembered many a child having rings on their legs after a long Winter of wellies as they called them, she had worn them but didn't like them as they always felt cold. Putting those thoughts to one side she smiled at her little girl and told her that the boots were gorgeous. It was now nearly May so she wouldn't be wearing them for very long anyway. You can bring them down to granny and grandad's farm next weekend and I'm sure uncle Pat will be glad of some help around the yard. Is it mucky down there asked Kate, Lily says it's always mucky around their farm. Who is Lily asked a puzzled Mary, that's my new friend announced Kate, she lives on a farm with her mummy and her brothers, she doesn't have a daddy, he is in Heaven, so her mummy is the farmer. She is getting first Communion too, but she doesn't have a dress yet because her mummy doesn't have much time for shopping. When we were in Mrs Canny's shop we saw a lovely white dress Mummy and Mrs Canny told daddy that if we wanted it for me we would have to put something on it I think it was a dep something, George laughed at his very vocal little daughter, It was a deposit Kate, She really fell in love with the dress Mary, said George sheepishly as he knew that Mary would realise that he could never say no to Kate. I did tell her that you would have the final say he told his wife but there is only one and we didn't want it to be sold by the time you got over there. Mary laughed at them both, she was just glad that George knew enough about the importance of the white dress to give out to them. I will go over to Canny's after tea and we will see if this dress is as nice as you say Kate. Mary was delighted to hear Kate prattle on about her new friend and the fact that there was no complaint about school this week. She would indeed go over to meet Mrs Canny and finalise the deal on the dress.

Mary and Kate were ready and waiting on Tuesday evening when Sally and Terence Sheehan arrived at the door, It was almost seven Thirty so they hurried on up

26

the hill to the school, Kate of course had seen Terence in the second class desk at school, he always sat on the end, she had also seen him in the school yard, he was always by himself in the corner playing a with a stick or talking to himself, he didn't join with the other boys kicking the ball around. She had thought he looked as lonely as she was, but now she had a friend and she would be seeing her at the meeting. Say hello to Terence her mother said giving her a little nudge, Hello Kate said shyly, Terence went bright red as his mother told him to shake hands. Kate decided there and then that she liked Terence, he would never kick a mucky ball at her and since she was not lonely anymore, she didn't want anyone else to be lonely either. Do you want to sit with me and Lily at the meeting she asked him, Terence was so taken aback by this unexpected friendly overture that he said yes before he got time to think about it. That's good then said Kate, come on, let's go, lets catch Lily and she ran off pulling Terence by the hand as he ran to keep up with her. Sally had tears in her eyes as she watched her different little boy go off with Kate, Are you ok Mary asked, she was proud of her daughter as she had always taught her to be kind to others, He is such a good little boy Sally sighed but I think he is going to have a hard time in this world of ours, He want's a white outfit like the girls for First Communion and Tom will go mad when he hears it she said sadly. They were at the school by now and no more was said. Father Hoey was standing at the door together with his Curate Father Jim Shine. The two priests were as different as chalk and cheese but jogged along well enough to keep

27

the flock of the Parish in order. Welcome, Boomed Fr. Hoey, This is Mrs Hill, she has just come from England to live here, he bestowed her a look that said and all of her funny English ways along with her, Nice to meet you, Father Jim said putting out his hand to Mary, she immediately felt here was someone that she could talk to if she ever needed a word of advice. As there were only six children in the First Communion class and Miss Conlon and the other parents were present Fr. Hoey took to the front of the room. Mary took a quick glance around and noted with a sigh of relief that there were no fathers present. She also took note of the little girl with the long pigtails sitting beside Kate with Terence on the other side. There was one other little girl and two boys who kept trying to shove each other of the end of the long wooden bench. The children will go to their first Confession next month Father Hoey boomed and there will be a special Saturday put aside for that. We will have one more meeting before the actual day and I need the children's baptismal certificates to be brought to that meeting. He droned on for a further thirty minutes before declaring that the meeting was over.

Chapter Three

Mary was packing the case for the trip down to Dufflin, it was the very same case that she had packed all those years ago when herself and Molly Mc Gee had made their sudden decision to stay in England. Every year boat loads of Irish people immigrated to either England or America, Mary's sister Meg had been the first to leave the Quinn Family homestead, she went to their mothers sister in Connecticut and was quickly followed by her brother Dan. Mary remembered the crying and lamenting that went on before they left and her Mammy saying when Dan left that will be the last of this family going anywhere Pat will have the farm and Mary will be educated and get herself a good job and a good husband. As Mary was only four when Meg left and six when Dan followed that in her eyes, they were mostly people who wrote letters home. Meg wrote every week for years after she left and her mother had a trunk full of those treasured epistles of life in America for the siblings. Dan wasn't much of a letter writer but he knew what Meg was writing each week as she made him listen, sometimes she also made him write a line or two at the bottom of the page. Mary also knew that when Pat was in his late teens Dan sent him the fare to come and join him but Pat knew his father was getting old and that his mother's heart would break. He kept the money in a tin box under his bed and wrote to thank Dan telling him he would think about it. Mary was sent to the local Convent school with money carefully saved up from the egg sales. The travelling shop called to Dufflin every Thursday and Annie Quinn carefully saved the egg money for Mary's education. They think I'm going to be a solicitor or a High Court Judge or something moaned Mary to her friend Molly as they ate their lunch in the Convent yard. Molly was really the one with the brains but her parents didn't really seem to care what she did. Her father was a busy doctor who never had a minute to think about anything other than his too many patients Her mother was always complaining about her health and the state of her hair and nails plus the many things that had no place for the prattle of a teenage daughter. Molly thought that she would like to be a nurse, while Mary had no clue where she wanted life to take her. The most pressing thought in their heads at that time had been the dance in the village of Kilmacaden on the last Friday of each Month. They were both going to be eighteen in June and thought it was about time that they were allowed to go to the dance. The leaving Cert would be over and hopefully they would do well. They talked incessantly about how the permission would be given until Mary had a brainwave, I will ask Pat to ask Mammy and daddy if we can go with him, he always gives in to me and you can tell your parents that you are coming with us, maybe your parents will let you stay in our house afterwards. They were bursting with excitement as the carefully thought out plan came to fruition. Pat didn't mind the girls coming with him and as he told his mother there wasn't much harm could come to them. They can't leave the hall until it's over he said as Father Murphy keeps a beady eye on the door and sure I 'll be there too.

Molly's mother never batted an eyelid when Molly said she would like to go to the dance on Friday night and stay over at Quinns afterwards. She did think distastefully about the clodhoppers that would be dancing with her daughter, but it was all too much to have to think about her daughter's life when she had so much stuff to worry about in her own. Molly didn't even tell her father as he wasn't there anyway. She took the shilling that it took to get into the dance out of the money jar on the mantlepiece and went to pack her nightdress, her blouse and her new blue drindle skirt for the dance.She also took a small bottle of Tweed perfume and a pink lipstick from her mother's dressing table She stuffed them into her satchel on Friday morning and met an excited Mary at the school gates. The girls could hardly contain themselves all day as they sat through double maths, history, geography and English. Oh my God said Molly as they tore out the gate and back to Quinns, I thought that day would never end. Annie Quinn had the dinner waiting for them as they burst in the door. Where is the fire she laughed as she welcomed Mary and the Doctor's daughter into the kitchen. She was proud of the fact that her lovely Mary had a friend of such high standing as the Doctor's daughter was a cut above the farming community. No such thoughts had ever entered the minds of the two girls as they had huddled together as nervous first year girls, five years ago in the Convent assembly hall, and they had been firm friends ever since. Molly thought how nice it was in the Quinn's kitchen, with everybody sitting down to eat dinner together. Paddy and his son Pat had come in from the farmyard and were now in the back kitchen washing their hands before dinner. Molly looked at Pat Quinn with his lovely Auburn hair which was several shades darker than Mary's, it curled at the back of his neck and tumbled on to his forehead, he pushed it back impatiently, his long eyelashes framing his startling green eyes. Well girls, he said I hear I am to have the company of two beautiful women with me to the dance this evening. Molly nearly fainted with delight, how come she had never noticed how attractive Mary's brother was, she had seen him in the distance many times but was never in his proximity before. Well don't be thinking that you have to dance with us said Mary, we will be looking for handsome young fellows once we get in there. We just want to go along with you until we get in the door. Molly could have brained Mary, She would be happy to dance with Pat Quinn all night. Paddy Quinn laughingly remarked, well now girls don't be counting your chicken's before they are hatched, sure the hall will be full of beautiful girls all wanting to dance with Pat. Annie turned to her husband, now Paddy don't be teasing the girls let them behave with decorum and enjoy the night, and make sure you are there to bring them home Pat, Annie warned her son. Mary had a lovely white dress with little rosebuds around the neck and a pink belt, it was one of the many that her thoughtful sister had sent over from the States. She tried to tame her long curly red hair into some sort of order but gave up as it just went it's own unruly way,

Molly put on the blue drindle skirt with the stiff slip and the white blouse that had a matching blue collar. Her jet black hair fell in waves around her shoulders while the blue in her skirt brought out the blue in her eyes. God we are bloody gorgeous said Molly giggling as the two girls admired themselves in the wardrobe mirror in Mary's room, don't swear or we'll never get out of here said Mary nervously. Molly lowered her voice, I have something in my purse that we can't put on until we are out the door, it's a pink lipstick belonging to my mother. Oh God said Mary do you think we are brave enough to wear lipstick? Well it's a very light shade of pink and no one will hardly notice. Well, Mary said fearfully, Father Murphy went up to a girl at the dance last month and wiped the red lipstick off her mouth, I heard Pat telling Mammy that, when she was picking the news out of him like she does every month. Molly thought quickly ok maybe I will throw it away or we will never get out of the house again if we get caught. They collapsed giggling on the bed and went instead with the safe option of drowning themselves in Mrs Mc Gee's'' Tweed'' perfume. We'll just bite our lips to make them pink laughed Mary. They tore down the stairs and into the kitchen where Annie was putting the dishes on the dresser. Well now Paddy she said to her husband who was sitting at the fire in his socks after a long day out on the farm he, looked up sleepily from the heat of the turf, He did a double take when he looked at his red haired Mary, she was beautiful and so was the lovely girl along with her, Be God Annie is my white shirt clean.I think Ill go to the dance myself just to get a turn

33

out of these two beautiful dancers. Mary put her arms around her beloved father's neck sure you can dance with me anytime you like dad but not tonight. Tonight we are going to take the eyesight out of the male population of Kilmacaden. Molly was entranced at this family show of love and teasing while at the back of her mind she was thinking about Pat Quinn and how great it was to be going to the dance with him.

Pat was also taken aback by the appearance of the two girls when he finally arrived into the kitchen with his lovely Auburn hair curled around his ears, his blinding white shirt, courtesy of his mother's scrubbing, and his jacket slung over his shoulder, Won't I be the envy of every fellow at the hall tonight he said to his mother swinging her round the room, stop your daft nonsense and put me down laughed Annie as she secretly enjoyed the good humoured banter of her handsome son. You make sure you look after these two and bring them home yourself, no going off with the lads remember. Stop worrying mother dear 'll mind them like gold dust he laughed as putting an arm around each of them he marched them out the door. Molly almost fainted at the feel of Pat's arm around her slender waist, she wished she could walk the whole way to the Parish hall tucked under Pats arm, but he let go of them when they got out the door. The night was warm and they chatted away as they took the half a mile walk into Kilmacaden.

Father Murphy stood at the small table at the Village hall door, he looked up in surprise as Pat Quinn arrived with the two girls in tow. Are these girls old enough to be going dancing he tackled Pat. Indeed and they are Father sure they are both eighteen he lied. Mary felt herself shrink in horror as Pat lied so easily to his reverence just imagine if they didn't get in after all the excitement. Here's the three shillings Father he said placing the coins on the table, Fr Murphy knew when he was beaten and Pat knew that he was not going to take a chance on the money being taken back. Go on in so he said and there is to be no leaving the hall until going home time. Of course not Father said Pat grinning and marching the two girls up the floor. Oh Pat said Mary, you lied to Father Murphy, we will all go to hell, sure you'll be eighteen before I go to Confession again Pat laughed, now go off and enjoy, but behave yourselves.

Chapter Four

The car was packed at last for the visit to Mary's parents, are we going for a night or for a month asked George as he tried to pack in Kate's wellingtons that had almost been left behind. Mary laughed you will be glad of the extra clothing and bedding when we get there and Kate will probably have to be changed every half hour, Why Mummy will I be meeting people all day asked Kate? no dear, but you are bound to get dirty if you are going to help Uncle Pat on the farm. Will I get to meet the cows and the chickens as soon as we get there she asked excitedly, well it will probably be dark and you will see them all tomorrow but Ginger the cat always sits beside the fire at night so you will get to see him. The neighbours will all call at some time tomorrow to see us, why will the neighbours be coming to see us asked George glancing at Mary askance. All of these people knew me before I went away and what I had for my breakfast, how often I sneezed and what time I went to bed at and they will want to see how I am and to see the handsome husband and daughter I have grinned Mary, They will want to know if you are good enough for me she teased. George was affronted, he thought to himself about the neighbours in Leeds where his parents lived and how he didn't even know them except to nod if they met on the Street. Do not mention that we weren't married in a Church or that you don't go to Mass she had told George before they left the house, I will explain everything to my mother and hope that she will tell my dad when she catches her breath. Will granny and granddad like me asked Kate, what if they don't understand what I am saying, do they like the King or can I not mention him she said as she thought of Miss Conlon's horror at the thought of having to Save him, where do they get the water from if they don't have taps, Do they have a shed for a lavatory, are they very old and sore, has uncle Pat any children? Mary listened in apprehension as she realised she had been so focused on George's religion or lack of it that she hadn't prepared Kate for anything at all. Granny and granddad are old but they are not at all sore, they will love you very much and so will uncle Pat. Mary thought how sad it was for her parents that their other grandchildren, lived across the Atlantic in America, Meg had a son and a daughter with her American husband Buddy, and Dan had one daughter with his Irish American wife Joyce. Kate would be the first sight of a grandchild for them and Mary knew that they would love her to bits.

Annie and Paddy Quinn were out the door as soon as they heard the car coming up the lane, they were sprightly enough for their age and were so looking forward to seeing their daughter and her family. They were still coming to terms with the fact that their daughter had left Ireland on that day so long ago and now she was married and to an English man at that. George was first out of the car and he went round to open the door for Mary which was noted by Paddy who thought well now isn't this a fine gentleman to be opening doors for my Mary who by now was out and helping the beautiful Blonde child from the back seat. A rush of hugs tears and kisses took place with George looking on as Mary finally pulled him into the hug, this is my husband mammy and daddy and this is my little girl Kate. Kate hung back behind her daddy as she looked at the people who were her grandparents. Well now aren't you the dote said Paddy Kate wasn't sure whether a dote was a good thing or a bad thing but her grandad was smiling at her, so it must be good. Just then Pat came around the side of the house, Mary was surprised at how good he looked, the years had been kind to him and he looked much as he had when she left. Here is your uncle Pat, Kate she said as she ran to hug her brother. George immediately liked the Auburn haired man who was his brother-in-law. They shook hands and Pat welcomed him to Dufflin. Mother of God said Annie will ye come on into the house and have the tea what are we thinking, having ye standing out in the yard, she led the way into the parlour as Mary realised they were now officially visitors. The Parlour was only ever used for Priests, visitors, Christmas and when they were having the Station. The table had the good tablecloth on, the one that had the crochet around the hem, that Mary remembered from her childhood and was set with the best tea set and an array of cakes and sandwiches. Sure the kitchen would have been grand Mammy, we didn't want to putting you to all this trouble. The room smelled damp and the fire of turf in the grate was just beginning to make an impression into heating the seldom used parlour. Mary gasped when she saw the electric light bulb hanging from the ceiling in the parlour. You never told me that you got the electricity,

we kept is as a surprise for when you would come said
Annie, we did indeed get it even though your father had
so many objections, it would cost a fortune to get a bulb
in each room, too many sockets would set the house on
fire, he also thought it would be too bright for us and
damage our eyesight and that we'd all go blind her
mother laughed,, we also have a bathroom upstairs
with running water coming out of taps she declared
with great pride and there is a tap in the back kitchen
where the men can wash their hands, and there is a
boiler yoke at the back of the range in the kitchen that
makes the water hot. Mary digested this wonderful
news as George who had hot water and Electricity at his
fingers tips all his life listened in astonishment at how
much this information touched him. He realised that
Mary's parents were so happy to be telling their
daughter how much this step up in the world meant to
them and he understood a little better of her fears of
hurting these lovely gentle people.

That is great news Mammy, Mary said as she struggled
to get her head around the fact that she was only in this
house for a visit. As soon as she came in the door, it was
as if she had never gone away, she was back being her
father's red haired Mary and the younger sister of Pat
who used to tease her and pull her hair. She was the
Mary who went reluctantly to the Convent each day to
learn everything that the nuns could teach her. She
remembered the evenings slogging over the dreaded
French verbs in the dimly lamp lit kitchen, What good
will French verbs be to me she moaned, whist child isn't
it the lucky girl you are to be learning a foreign language

sure you never know when it will be useful, Mary looked at her mother in disbelief, where did she think she would be using it, Had the man who drove the travelling shop suddenly become bilingual ?did the butcher in the village suddenly acquire a knowledge of French, Mammy who would never be learning anything new and had nothing to worry about except the price of the eggs looked at her daughter with love and admiration. Oh how innocent she was back then not realising that her mother was the backbone of the farm, that she kept the men and the farm house in ticking over with her washing and scrubbing, with the milking and calving of the cows, when the men were out in the fields. She never complained all the while Mary was moaning even though she must be tired and weary of the nature of her days. She was broken hearted when Mary and Molly announced that they were getting the boat to England that Summer for a for what was supposed to be a two-week holiday in St. Bernard's Convent with Molly's cousin the nun. They had both done very well in their leaving cert and Molly's father had expected his daughter to follow him in the medical profession by going off to train for nursing. Mary's parents weren't too sure where she could go to get a good job. Neither of them were expected to go any further with their education. Mary thought she would like to work in a library as she loved books and reading. Fr Murphy had called to say that the solicitors in town were looking for a girl to train up in the office and that Mary should try for it. Mary knew that if Fr. Murphy said she should try for it, then that is what she would be doing as her mother thought of him as the fountain of Knowledge. Molly had applied for nursing in Dublin and was looking forward to getting away. Mary had been hoping to get away with her to work in Dublin but that chance seemed to be fading away with the job coming up in Lynch and Downey Solicitors. Maybe I should do a terrible interview she said to Molly as they sat on the stump of a tree at the edge of Backwood forest. The July sun was shining warmly on their bent heads as the discussed their plans for the future. You wouldn't know how to said Molly grinning, she knew that Mary wanted to get away from Dufflin, while she would love to stay there forever, she had fallen madly in love with Pat Quinn and didn't want to leave at all. The night of the dance had been wonderful, Pat came up to the girls and asked them how it was going, go away hissed Mary or we will never get a dance. I would like the pleasure of this dance Miss Molly Mc Gee he said ignoring Mary's horrified Face, leave her alone Mary said shoving him to one side, but Molly was already taking Pat's hand and heading on to the dance floor. The band were playing ''Danny Boy'' and forever more Molly had only to close her eyes when she heard that song and she was back in Pat Quinn's arms. Pat was surprised by how well Molly could dance, you are a dark horse he said as he skilfully steered her around the floor. I learned to dance at my cousin's birthday party in Dublin last Summer she told him as she looked up into his green eyes. Pat was a bit taken aback by the feeling he got from having this lovely girl in his arms, she was his little sister's best friend, he couldn't play fast and loose with her as often did with

41

the many girls who had fallen for his charms. She was as light as a feather on her feet and for the first time in his life Pat was sorry when the dance was over, he reluctantly let her go and astonished himself as he whispered into her ear, save the last dance for me. He knew that she liked him by the way she was looking at him and he gave himself a talking to as he walked down the hall, she is a kid, she is Mary's friend there are lots of girls here willing to take my arm, what is it about this one he thought. He came to a halt as the band started playing a quick step and Cissy O' Shea stepped out in front of him, He knew she was after him and he took her arm as he asked her to dance. Cissie was delighted with herself as Pat swung her around the floor. He pulled her close as they came to the corner at the door and just as Father Murphy walked out to move them apart, No close dancing if you please and don't even be thinking of going outside Pat Quinn, the Priest barked as he moved on to the next couple, Pat grinned as he thought to himself that is exactly what he had been intending, to get Cissie outside for a quick kiss, Close dancing and too much familiarity was very much frowned upon by Father Murphy and the Catholic Church in general and he made sure no such carry on, as he called it took place in his Parish. Mary was having the time of her life as she was the belle of the ball and was totally exhausted and exhilarated as she was swung from one partner to the next. The girls met up between dances and declared it was the best night of their lives. Molly saw Pat going by with Cissie O' Shea and was surprised by the jealous streak that came over her. She pushed the jealous thoughts out of her head and instead remembered Pat's whispered "Save the last dance for me". The next dance was a lady's choice and the girls dithered about whether they would be bold enough to ask any one out to dance. Molly watched Cissie flying along the hall until she came to Pat and pulled him on to the dance floor, she decided there and then that she wasn't going to ask any fellow, I am sitting this one out she told Mary as she sat down Mary was feeling tired after all the leaping about and she also sat down, they watched as the girls in their Summer dresses floated by to a slow waltz. Molly watched Pat and Cissie out of the corner of her eye, Pat had his head thrown back and was laughing at something Cissie said. Molly's heart lurched uncomfortably somewhere in the region of her shoes. The last dance was announced and a mad dash of fellows from one side of the hall to the side where the girls were ensued. Mary was grabbed by Jim Collins who lived in the next farm to theirs, while Molly looked in desperation to see if Pat was coming to claim her, she could see Jim Collins twin brother Johnny heading towards her, she looked down at her feet pretending not to see him when she was suddenly swept off into the last waltz. Pat Quinn was laughing down at her as they floated along. At least Molly thought that was what they were doing., She was in Heaven. Immediately afterwards at twelve o'clock Sharp the band played the National Anthem and as everyone stood to attention Molly thought her heart would burst at the feelings it was having as she stood between Pat and Mary. They collected their coats from the cloakroom and went to the door where everyone was milling around while Father Murphy did his best to segregate the women from the men. Pat took the girls by the elbows and marched them through the throng. They giggled as the priest frowned at this show of bravado. Off home with you now Quinn he boomed and take care of the girls. I will indeed father said Pat as he irreverently pulled his forelock. Once they were outside Pat let them go and Mollie felt bereft as she was enjoying the touch of Pat's hand on her elbow. Cissie O' Shea was waiting for Pat as they came down the lane from the Hall, she took him by the arm, well Pat Quinn, I will let you walk me home if you are a good boy she laughed as she looked up at him with a glint in her eye. Mary and Molly were shocked at this blatant display of forwardness, Mary 's mother had done her best to explain that men liked to make the first move and that a lady should wait to be asked. Cissie seemed to have no such boundaries as she laughingly pulled Pat away from the girls. Well now he said much and all as the pleasure that would give me, I am otherwise engaged tonight, my mother would never let me back into the house again if I abandoned these young ladies. Mollie breathed again as she had been holding her breath since Cissie had asked Pat to take her home. She was going home with Pat Quinn, she would probably see him at breakfast, she was in Heaven. Cissie was none to pleased at this turn of events and she sulkily turned her back on Pat and made her way back up to the Hall. I suppose I'll have to go home with my brother so, she said darkly glaring at Pat. Pat laughed and once again took the girls by an arm each as they sauntered off back to Dufflin in the moonlit night. That Cissie O' Shea is a brazen hussy said Mary looking at her brother in disapproval, you should keep away from her, Pat laughed at this sisterly giving out he was getting, now Mary, he grinned I didn't notice you pulling away from young Jimmy Collins at the old time waltz he remarked while Mary felt herself go hot round the cheeks, she had indeed enjoyed being held closely by Jim Collins when Fr. Murphy had his back turned. Well I Won't tell if you don't she said to her brother who was enjoying teasing his little sister. Molly meantime was lost in a fantasy of dreams, she was walking down the Aisle with Pat Quinn in a beautiful white dress, She had a gold ring on her finger and she was Mrs Quinn, Isn't that right Molly, Pat Said giving Molly's arm a gentle squeeze, Molly awoke from her dreaming with a start, what 's right she said looking through the moonlight at Pat through her long lashes, don't tell me you are dreaming about the other twin Collins he laughed looking down at Molly, she was horrified at the thought and said so in such a fierce voice that Pat laughed and putting his arms around her twirled her around and said to her eternal embarrassment, don't be wasting your time on that young fellow, wait until you grow up and you can come out with me. Neither Pat nor Molly could credit the words that he had just uttered, Pat was thunderstruck at himself, he who never gave any girl a second thought and now he was moving in on his sister's friend. What in Heaven's name was wrong with him. As for Molly she didn't know if she was insulted at the thought of being

45

told she wasn't a grown up or elated at the fact that Pat wanted to go out with her. Mary in the meantime was sick of all this nonsense, she wanted to get home to bed, come on she said let's run the rest of the way and she took off like a bat out of hell up the lane to the farmhouse. Pat for once in his life wasn't sure what to do, so he took Molly in his arms and kissed her gently on the mouth, you can remember this night he said looking down at her and your first kiss. Goodnight my lovely Molly he said to the young girl by his side who was almost fainting. They reached the farmhouse and Molly ran as if her life depended on it, she tore up the stairs after Mary and fell on the bed in a frenzy of delight. Mary looked at her in astonishment what's up she said looking at Molly's flushed face and red cheeks. Oh Mary she said I'm in love. Mary looked at her friend in disbelief, oh my God is it that awful Johnny Collins or that eejit Tom Cane, it can't possibly be Fr. Murphy, who are you in love with, tell me before I burst. Molly took a deep breath, It's Pat she said dreamily, Pat who, said Mary I didn't see any Pat there worth falling in love with. Molly looked at her friend, it's your Pat she said, your brother Pat. Mary fell down on the bed beside Molly looking at her as if she had sprouted two heads, are you crazy she yelled, he's my brother, he's old and he's always teasing girls you can't be in love with him.

But in love she was and for the rest of the Summer Molly spent more time at the Quinns house than she did at her own, she didn't have the wiles of Cissie O Shea in the art of courtship, all she knew was that had Pat asked her to go to the moon she would have gone. Mary was appalled at this love sickening change in her friend, you are not in love with my brother, you just think you are, he is too old for you, you have not met any other men how can you fall for the first one that looks at you. Molly thought about Mary's words of wisdom but it didn't make any difference. Pat was so used to seeing Molly at the house now that he began to have a much greater feeling towards the young girl, because that's what he thought she was, a young girl, Mary's friend, but he knew that the feelings that had crept up on him were not the feelings one had for a young girl but the feelings for a young women. Pat was notorious for the amount of broken hearts he had left scattered around the Parish, while none of them had made any impression on his own and he never gave any of them a second thought, Molly had dug herself into his heart. To be fair to him he fought his feelings and avoided Molly for a time but it was no good, she was in his head morning, noon and night. The next month's dance was to be the last but one before Molly left for her nurses training and the holiday in England. Mary would be starting in the Solicitor's office in September and their lives were set out before them. I will probably die an old maid in that office and will be found buried beneath a pile of dusty old files she complained to Molly as they sat on the grassy mound looking down over the farm. The sun was hot on their backs and Molly looked at her friend guiltily. She had been meeting Pat secretly all Summer, when ever they got a chance, they had held hands and kissed passionately, Father Hoey would have been horrified. Pat was also feeling guilty as he worked

47

in the top meadow and looked over at the girls in sitting in the long grass. He couldn't explain the feelings he had for Molly, they had taken him over eight years isn't that big of a difference he told himself, but in experience he knew it was, Molly had none, she was barely left school, he didn't know how he would feel if Mary was with someone his age. He would try and explain it to Molly when they went to the dance on Friday, he would let her go, see the world and maybe she would come back to him. Time would tell and he would feel the better man for letting her go. Or so he told himself. The girls that got ready for the dance on the Friday night were a little subdued but they still had the holiday in England to look forward to in seven weeks time.

Chapter Five

The night of the dance came and the girls got ready, they felt themselves to be so much more sophisticated since the first dance, they were both now eighteen ready to face the World. Mary hoped Jim Collins would be at the dance, he was very nice, but not someone she would ever consider as husband material, he was a farmer, for God's sake, she didn't intend to get bogged down in milking cows, saving hay and saving the egg money to supplement her income for the rest of her life. She was going to work in the solicitors Office until she had enough money to get out of the dreaded dullness of Dufflin and away to the bright lights of somewhere, anywhere. She wondered why they called it the bright lights, maybe because the streets had lights along the pavement not like at home where you stumbled along like a blind man. Molly on the other hand was happy and sad, she really wanted to be a nurse but she couldn't bear the thought of leaving Pat Quinn to the wily clutches of Cissie O'Shea but tonight she would enjoy the dance and forget about everything else. Father Murphy had a slight chill according to the curate Fr. Mc Gowan who had left the Parish priest's Housekeeper dosing him with hot whiskey, lemon and cloves. Fr. Mc Gowan was young and not as uptight as the Parish priest about keeping the segregation rules at the Parish dance, he also liked to smoke the odd ''Woodbine'' or two and could be seen sticking his head in behind the coat rack as he pursued this sinful habit as

Father Murphy called it. Close dancing went into a frenzy as each puff of the cigarette was enjoyed by the Curate and more sins and bad thoughts were committed during the smoking sessions than at all of the previous dances overlooked by Fr. Murphy. Molly was in Pat's arms, he pulled her closer than he ever had before and pulled her head in to his as they danced cheek to cheek, Mary was also dancing cheek to cheek with Jim Collins as was almost every other couple in the hall, Mary didn't actually like the feel of Jim's one day growth of beard, she just liked the idea of dancing in the forbidden closeness. Pat Quinn didn't like the fact that he was going to have to tell Molly that their romance, if it could be called that would have to stop. He knew it was for the best, for her sake and for the sake of his own sanity. He looked over at Mary dancing cheek to cheek with Jim Collins and knew that if Jim had thoughts in his head towards Mary like the ones he was having about Molly, he would have beaten the living day lights out of him. The dance finished and so did the smoking session in the cloakroom, couples hastily pulled apart and everything went back to Normal. Mary came up to Pat and looking at him pleadingly said, Jim would like to walk me home, but only if you say it's ok, we will walk in front of you and Molly so you can see us but don't come too close she warned. Pat thought quickly, Jim Collins was a good lad and he knew he could trust him with his sister, he also thought it would be a good opportunity to talk to Molly alone. After pretending to ponder the question he nodded his head, I will agree, you can walk ahead of us but there is to be no hanky panky he

50

grinned. Mary shoved him playfully, I don't really need your permission, I am eighteen and I do have a mind of my own, it was Jim's idea that I ask for it. Pat 's estimation of Jim Collin's rose considerably at that and his mind was at ease, his mother (and Father) would kill him if anything untoward happened to his sister. Go on ahead so he nodded, Molly and myself will follow at a discreet distance he said taking Molly by the arm. Mary scampered off to the red faced young man who was waiting bashfully for her at the door. Cissie O' Shea passed by on the arm of a man that Molly had often seen at her father's surgery, oh my God she thought it's one of those solicitor's that Mary is going to work for, John Downey, that's it he must be about a hundred , what is he doing at the Parish dance, what was wrong with Cissie, she looked at Pat to see how he was taking this but he wasn't even looking he was concentrating on what he was going to say to make this easier. Mary and Jim were gone ahead walking while Mary talked nineteen to the dozen, she was telling him about the trip to England while he listened with envy, he would love to get away too but he knew the possibility was most unlikely. Pat took Molly's arm as they slowly followed his sister and Jim Collins, Molly darling he said there is something I'must say to you, Molly looked up at him and he was swamped in her loving look, they were almost out of the light that was outside of the village hall and he knew if they were in the dark and he couldn't really see her, it would be easier. She trustingly put her hand in his and thought about how happy she was at that moment. It was now impossible to see Mary and Jim and as they came to Meehan's hayshed, where they had often met up over the Summer, Molly took the usual turn in, deep in thought Pat followed her, they would be away from prying eyes and he could let her down gently. He took her in his arms and started to talk but her mouth was much closer than he thought and his lips automatically closed down on hers. Oh god he groaned to himself this was not supposed to happen suddenly they were on the hay and Pat and Molly were lost in the haze of romance and pent up frustration. It happened as it did in so many others in hay sheds all over the Country. Pat was disgusted with himself afterwards not because he didn't enjoy the lovely experience but because he had done the exact opposite of what he had planned. Molly moved in his arms and sighed, she had never felt so loved or so guilty in her life. What had happened was not the way she wanted to give herself to Pat, she wanted to be Mrs Pat Quinn before such liberties took place. She felt him move beside her as he sat up and said to her horror, that must never happen again, I am so sorry Molly I took advantage of you and I will never forgive myself. I brought you in here to tell you that we must stop seeing each other, Molly was struck dumb and as she tried to protest, nothing came out of her mouth, You are too young, you haven't seen the world, you are going to get away and become a great nurse, you will meet lots of fine young men and will forget all about me. He continued on and on while Molly became more frantic with despair. Finally she found her voice, I love you Pat I would never have done what we have if I didn't, I don't even want to go away, I want to stay near you. Pat talked to her gently, I am too old for you Molly my darling girl, I want you to see the world to get away and live a different life to what you have here, your father would kill me if he knew what had just happened and I wouldn't blame him. Moly knew that was true but the only thing that registered in her head was the fact that Pat had called her his darling girl. She felt sick at the thought of what they had done and knew that she couldn't face Mary tonight. Please take me back to my own house she whispered her white face looking up at Pat in the moonlight, tell Mary that I felt sick and that Ill talk to her tomorrow. Pat nodded his head as he led the shattered girl out of the hayshed. They walked the few hundred yards to the bottom of Quinns lane and Pat shouted out to Mary to go on in that Molly was going home to her house as she didn't feel well. You can come with us he beckoned to Jim Collins who had hastily dropped his arm from around Mary when he saw Pat appear. Mary waved as she ran into the house and three forlorn figures made their way back to Collin's farm gate where Jim muttered a goodnight and the other two made their way to the Doctor's house which stood up a driveway beside the village Church. Pat opened his mouth to say something to Molly about the fact that he would wait for her if she still wanted to come back to him, but she didn't give him a chance she ran up the driveway and disappeared before he had a breath taken. She ran around to the back door which was beside the surgery, the light was on and she could see her father still inside, probably back from a late night call, she skirted around the surgery and in the back door, her mother would be in bed she knew as she made her way up to the bathroom. The doctor's house was one of the few in the village that had electricity and running water, Molly knew that there probably wasn't any hot water, but she didn't care, she ran the lukewarm bath and got in, her tears mixing with the tepid water. My heart is broken, I will never look at another man as long as I live, I wish I never met Pat Quinn she sobbed quietly to herself. She had broken one of the strictest rules of the Catholic Church, sex before marriage was a mortal sin, she would go to hell., she could never go to confession again because Father Murphy would come out of the confessional and throttle her, she would be shamed for ever.

Molly now realised that she would be glad to get away to Dublin. She wished they didn't have to go on the holiday to England because she knew Mary would pick the secret out of her. They had been friends for so long and each knew what the other was thinking. I did it she thought and the sky didn't fall but I am so ashamed that the loving feeling that I had was wiped out when Pat said he didn't want to see me anymore. I will never give myself to an other man, maybe I ll become a nursing nun she sobbed as she got out of the bath in which the water was by now stone cold, shivering Molly towelled herself dry and got into her nightie, she thought she wouldn't sleep, but she fell into an exhausted slumber almost as soon as her head hit the pillow. She didn't wake until she heard Mary shouting at her from the landing, get up you lazy lump, Molly Mc Gee its nearly eleven o' clock. Molly lifted her head blearily from the pillow, she felt bruised and sore, and of course her heart was broken but she would have to put on a brave face, or at least until they got out of the house. I 'll be down in a minute, wait for me in the kitchen, Mam always goes to get her hair done on Saturday morning and there is no one there, put on the kettle she mumbled through the door. She listened as she heard Mary bounding down the stairs, She shuffled into her clothes like an old woman and as she looked into the bathroom mirror she thought she could see sinner stamped on her forehead. She shook herself and straightened her back as she slowly made her way downstairs, she could hear Mary singing to herself as she waited for the kettle to boil. Mary was full of the joys of life, she didn't even look at Molly as she poured the boiling water into the teapot, Molly, she said gleefully, guess what, Jim Collins kissed me last night. Molly's face turned a bright red as she tried to look away from Mary's excited prattle, how I wish that is all that I did she thought as she took the mug of tea from Mary, Her tongue was stuck to the roof of her mouth as she tried to say something, anything to get Mary off that certain subject. Her friend looked at her in surprise, are you still sick she asked looking closely at Molly's blotchy face. Molly couldn't have answered to save her life, Mary, who knew her friend so well asked tentatively, did something happen last night, did my brother do anything to harm you. Molly burst out crying, no, I'mean yes, no, not really. Mary stared at Molly in consternation, what did Pat do, did he kiss you?

All Molly's pent up emotion and relief at letting her friend know that Pat had kissed her many times over the Summer burst out of her mouth as she suddenly couldn't stop talking. Mary I have been seeing Pat all during the summer she gasped and I love him so much, I thought he loved me but now I don't know anymore and he doesn't want to see me again. He says I'm too young and that I should go out and see the world and live a bit of life. Mary, she sobbed we got carried away I let him do something last night that I will regret for the rest of my life. Mary looked in astonishment at Molly and with her mouth agape she gasped... you didn't go the whole way with Pat did you? She looked at Molly's downcast face and started to rant and rage at her brother who lucky for him wasn't anywhere near her. What is wrong with you she shouted at Molly, you could have a baby, The words had left her lips before she thought and Molly's renewed burst of weeping began like a waterfall that couldn't be controlled. Mary suddenly felt sorry for her friend and furious with her brother, We will get out of here she said, we will go to England and have a wonderful holiday, of course you Won't have a baby she comforted Molly, you only did it once, she said looking at her for confirmation, Oh God yes, we never did anything only kiss before. You will put Pat out of your head and we will find two lovely English fellows who will be so polite that we will have to beg them to kiss us Mary said trying to cheer Molly up, she did get a glimmer of a smile as she wiped her friends tears away with the tea towel. Come on get yourself tidied up and we will enjoy the rest of the Summer, we will go and decide what we are going to pack for the holiday, I will bring my case down here and leave it in your bedroom so you don't have to look at my traitor of a brother. Molly grabbed Mary's arm in a vice like grip, you must promise me never to tell anyone and you must especially promise never to say anything to Pat about last night Mary, who had every intention of giving Pat a piece of her mind, had to back down. Okay I promise she said before Molly left an imprint of her fingers on her arm for ever.

Chapter Six

The few weeks went quickly and the girls got ready for the boat trip to England, They were sailing from Dublin on the Tuesday, The Convent was in Buckinghamshire and they were getting a train from Holyhead to Windsor. At this stage Molly was almost sure that she was indeed going to have a baby.she hadn't had her period and she was always on time, she felt different and had been sick in the mornings. She really wasn't looking forward to the boat trip over the rough Irish sea. She said nothing of this to Mary but packed as much of her clothes as she could into her suitcase because she knew without a doubt she wouldn't be coming back. She nursed her broken heart as best she could and told herself she was lucky to get this opportunity to get away without anyone knowing her situation. She had written one of the most difficult letters of her life to her cousin Sister Bernadette who was under pain of death to burn the letter and not to write back.

Molly told her that nobody knew and that she would do any work that needed to be done in the Convent if she could stay until the baby was born, after that she would decide where to go from there. She just couldn't think that far ahead. She knew she would eventually have to tell Mary, but kept putting it off. Mary was full of what they would do for the two weeks all the places that would visit. Places that they had only ever heard about. Molly didn't have the heart or the energy to put her off. Molly's dad was very happy that she was going to have a holiday before she started her nursing training, he gave her thirty pounds to spend in England, it was a small fortune to Molly and the only stipulation being that she would give something to Sister Bernadette and the nuns who were going to look after them for the few weeks. Her mother thought it was a good idea too, only she wished that she wasn't staying with those awful nuns who might encourage her daughter to join them. She shuddered at the thought but she would put that idea out of her head and concentrate on her own trip to Dublin and civilisation where she could get a decent haircut and buy herself some winter clothes. Molly's heart was breaking as she thought about her father who had no idea that he wouldn't see his daughter again for she now knew that she couldn't give up her baby and that she would never be able to come back to Kilmcaden.

The morning for England broke bright and sunny and Mary kissed her mother and father goodbye, see you in a few weeks she laughed happily as she lifted her suitcase up into the horse and trap. Her dad was leaving her to the station where they would get the train to Dublin, they were meeting Molly there as her dad was dropping her off on his way to do his sick calls. Mary was just about civil to Pat whom she and Molly had been avoiding for some time. Pat always seemed to be out on the farm his brow furrowed as he tried to put Molly out of his mind. He had half heartedly asked Cissie O' Shea to go to the cinema one night but she haughtily shook her head at him. I already have a date she said. Looking at him under her eyelashes, I am now walking out with John Downey of Lynch, Downey Solicitors and Co., she bragged. If she was hoping to get a response she was disappointed as Pat gave a sigh of relief, good woman so, he said walking off leaving her looking after him with her mouth open. She had hoped that Pat would be jealous and maybe think about marrying her but he seemed a million miles away. She knew she had John Downey where she wanted him, he had lots of money a good career and he wasn't that old Forty five at most and he was mad about her. He had been living with his mother until her recent death, hence the reason he was beginning to have a life. Pat was thinking about Molly and wishing that he could have that night back again and he never would have gone into Meehan's Hayshed. She was so pure and innocent and he had taken that away from her. He would never forgive himself. He wanted to tell her how sorry he was before she went away but had sense enough to know that this would be a bad idea. She would soon get over him, whether he would get over her was another thing. He knew that she had told Mary from the way she was also avoiding him and he felt terrible about that too as his sister had always looked up to him and he had always looked out for her. He waved to the trap as it passed him by in the farmyard, Mary half heartedly lifted her hand in a wave, she hated being nasty to Pat but she felt for her friend who was going around like a sick hen. She hoped the nuns would let them out of the Convent and let them have a good time, Annie Quinn stood at the door thinking the very opposite, sure the nuns Won't let them out much they will be safe as houses she thought waving the tea towel at Mary as she took off for England.

A very pale Molly stood at the Station house door as she waited for the Quinns to arrive. Her father had dropped her there as he was in a hurry to get to a sick call, she clung to him as if her life depended on it as he hugged her goodbye. Sure you're only going for the few weeks he laughed as he untangled himself from her hug. Molly didn't know how she stopped herself from bursting into tears, she grimaced at him with the best smile she could muster. She had committed the greatest crime in the eyes of the Church and there was no way that as an unmarried mother she could come back to her parents and Kilmacaden. She stood a forlorn figure in her brown tweed coat as Mary and Paddy Quinn trotted up in the horse and trap. Paddy lifted Mary's case down and handed it to her, Well girls he said, only for I know

Annie would kill me, I would go off to England with the two of you on this fine adventure. Paddy who had only been to Dublin once in his life to get his appendix out laughed at the idea of himself in London. Don't be talking to strangers now he advised the girls keep to yourselves and don't be telling anyone your business. Mary laughed, she had every intention of talking to all and sundry, she kissed her father on the cheek of course we will do what ever you say dad she said tongue in cheek, while even Molly smiled at the thought of Mary being quiet. They said goodbye to Paddy as the train puffed into the station, See you in a few weeks he shouted above the noise and clanking of the train. At last they were off, the journey to Dublin seemed to flash by like a shot as Mary chatted away to Molly, there was a fellow and a girl in their carriage who were obviously a new husband and wife from the way they were trying to behave as if they were married for years and not let on that they were newly weds. The girl couldn't stop looking at her left hand and it's shiny new wedding band, while he couldn't tear his eyes away from his lovely bride. There was also an elderly woman who was reading a book on nursing, as Molly found out when it got left on the seat beside her while the woman went to get something from her case in the overhead rack. Molly sadly thought of her own aspirations for a nursing career and choked back a sob as she felt it would never happen What would happen, she thought to herself as she heard Mary talking to the newly weds. She knew she wouldn't be coming back to Ireland and she also knew Mary would be horrified and sick to the stomach when she found out that she would have to travel back on her own. Molly hadn't really worked out yet what she reason she was going to give to her parents, her head ached at all the mad thoughts whirling around in it. Maybe she could say she was enchanted with the life in the Convent and that she heard a voice from God calling her to enter. Her mother would go mad while her gentle father would probably suggest that she become a nursing nun. She pretended to be asleep to avoid talking until the train pulled into the Station. There was a mad scramble of getting cases down from the racks, people yelling and shouting to each other as Molly and Kate tried to remember where they were going next, The woman with the book on nursing had told them she was travelling to Holyhead and they saw her head out of the station they quickly followed her. They knew they had to travel out to Kingstown to catch the boat and that the train to there was at another platform. They were safely on at last and Mary heaved a sigh of relief at the thought that the next train they took would be in Wales. She was so excited by the thought of the adventure ahead and couldn't figure out why Molly was so down in herself. Mary thought she should be over Pat by now and she tried to jolly her friend into some sort of semblance of excitement. Mary's joy at the trip was catching and Molly told herself off for being so miserable. She pulled herself together and smiled at her friend, come on then so lets get this holiday off the ground. Mary laughed, we will have the best time in England, we will have so much to see and do in the two weeks that you won't have time to think about my clown of a brother.

They were on the boat at last and as they looked at the Irish coast disappearing from view, they decided to go downstairs where it wouldn't be so windy. Molly was beginning to feel sick but didn't want to say anything to Mary as she wasn't sure if she was seasick or pregnant sick. She was going to have to tell her friend and now was as good a time as any. As long as she lived Molly Mc Gee would remember that Boat trip as the worst time in her life. She felt so ill on the crossing while Mary breezed through the whole thing. There were other passengers also looking as ill and bedraggled as Molly so she didn't really feel out of place but it was now or never, she had to tell her friend before they got to St. Bernard's. She pulled Mary down beside her on the wooden slatted seat as the boat tossed and turned over the Irish sea. Mary I have something very important to tell you and you must never tell anyone, Mary looked in astonishment at her friend's white face and took her cold hands in hers, Of course she whispered, what is it, are you not going to go back home, which in Mary's eyes was the only thing she could think of that could be so serious. Molly shook her black waves back from her clammy forehead and whispered back no I am not going back home …..ever. Mary looked at her in shock, is it that clown Pat that has you staying away, don't be thinking about him give him a shove out of your life, don't be daft of course you will come back home. Molly tearfully looked at Mary and whispered once more, I have put him out of my life but I am expecting his baby

63

and I can never go back. Mary was speechless, she was upset for Molly and furious all over again with Pat. She knew what she said next would have to be comforting for Molly. She put her arm around her friend and said staunchly, then I Won't go back either, we will get you through this and I will never let you down. Molly gratefully clung to Mary, thank you she said you are a friend in a million, but you can't stay in England there is no reason for you to, your mother would come over after you, both girls gave a weak smile at the thought of Annie Quinn boarding the boat and sailing over to England in full flight after her daughter. You and my cousin Sister Bernadette are the only ones that know Molly said and I have asked her to see if I can stay on there after the holiday. I told her not to answer me by letter, so I have to wait until I get there to see what the Reverend Mother says. Mary who by now was as white as Molly nodded her head, she was trying to imagine how Molly felt and knew instinctively that had the shoe been on the other foot Molly would stay with her. She said no more, resolving to wait until they got to the Convent to see how things would work out. They were both very quiet for the rest of the journey and both were worn out when they arrived at St. Bernard's Convent in Windsor.

Sister Bernadette met them at the door and took one look at the girls and ushered them into the visitor's parlour where tea and toast was waiting. As soon as you have eaten off to bed with you my dears Sister Bernadette announced, we will talk tomorrow. They were glad to obey and after eating a little they were brought upstairs through a long corridor and into a very nice room with two single beds a wardrobe and dressing table. The bathroom is next door and is only used by our visitors so you can wander in your dressing gowns Sister Bernadette told the girls. They were both exhausted and fell into the comfortable looking beds. Molly had the best night's sleep that she had for ages and felt much better when she woke up next morning. She looked over at the other bed which was empty as Mary was already enjoying the luxury of a bath. She arrived back full of the joys of life her red curly hair drying in the towel she was vigorously rubbing it with. How are you today she asked hoping that Molly would also be in good humour, she was glad to see that Molly was surprisingly happier than she had been for the past weeks. I'm not too bad at all I don't feel sick and I'm so glad to be on dry land. Mary laughed, go and have a nice long bath and I will get dressed and pick out your clothes for the day my lady, we will then eat and go out on the town. She was glad to see Molly nodding her head. When both girls were dressed they sat quietly on their beds both lost in thought until Sister Bernadette knocked on the door and ushered them down to the dining hall for breakfast. Most of the Nuns had eaten as they were always up early for Mass in the Convent Chapel. There was a school attached to the building and children's voices could be heard chattering away in the distance. The girls were touched to see the spread of breakfast food laid out for them, porridge, Bacon and eggs and a big pot of tea and toast. Thank you so much Norah, Molly said to her cousin reverting to her birth name, Sister Bernadette smiled it was so long since anyone had called her Norah it made her think of home, her parents, brothers and sisters and her favourite Aunt Norah after whom she was named. Oh I'm so sorry muttered Molly I will have to get used to saying Sister Bernadette, Don't be worrying about it said the nun smiling it was quite nice to hear my name from my old life again. What have you two girls planned for the day? Well said Mary, before Molly got a chance to open her mouth we would love to go and see Windsor Castle the River Thames and any suggestions that you have for us would be very welcome, of course we are going into London as well on one of the days. The nun nodded her head, I will write down an itinerary for you for all the wonderful things that you can see and do while you are here she said kindly, but first Molly I would like to take you to Reverend Mother for a little talk. Mary, we have some lovely grounds here with a beautiful kitchen garden and a walled flower garden, I have asked our gardener Willie to give you the guided tour while Molly and I go to see mother Agnes. She walked with the girls out of the refectory and through the pillared gate into the garden, where an old man was supervising the pulling of weeds.

Molly was feeling very well this morning and the sickness seemed to have abated, but it suddenly came back in force at Sister Bernadette's words. Molly I know you asked me not to divulge your secret, but here in St. Bernard's there are no secrets, Reverend Mother knows your story and she wishes to speak with you. Don't be afraid, as under that stern countenance mother is quite gentle. Molly 's sick feeling returned with a vengeance and her face was pale under her black fringe. I have done the spade work and asked if you can stay until the birth, continued Sister Bernadette but Mother wished to give you her answer herself. I will leave you in the visitor's parlour and she will be with you in five minutes. Molly sat down, the smell of beeswax and the vase of Roses on the table assailed her nostrils and as she sat waiting she remembered all the horror stories she had heard of girls who got into her situation, girls who were never allowed home again, where did there babies go, did any of them get to keep the poor little innocent beings. The thoughts were going around and around her head making her dizzy when a hand gently tapped her on the shoulder, she almost jumped out of her skin. Mother Agnes was tall, thin and serious looking, she spoke with a very slight Irish brogue which somehow was comforting to Molly. My dear, she spoke quietly with the voice that God seemed to have reserved for nuns, I have spoken with your cousin and she has told me your story and how you asked to stay with us until your baby is born, Yes please Mother, Molly whispered as her throat almost closed over with fright as she knew what the Nun said next would determine the next part of her life. I know that your parents would be so distressed at your predicament but I also know that a new life is to be cherished, I will tell you something that I have kept close to my heart for a very long time, I had a dearly loved older sister who loved a man as you did and when my parents found out, they and the Parish Priest decided that she would have to go away as if she was some sort of criminal, she was sent to a place for unmarried mothers in Galway and I never saw her again. I have no idea what happened to either her or her baby, we were never again allowed to speak her name. Her boyfriend ended his torture one night in the lake. God rest his soul. My sister's name was Agnes and that is why I took her name in religion and also why I will say to you my child, that you are welcome to stay her for as long as you like and that you and nobody else will decide your baby's future.

Molly was speechless at this display of unity and kindness, she gasped a great big lungful of air as she stuttered her thanks to the elderly Nun. She took out the thirty Pounds her father had given her and handed to the Reverend Mother. My father asked me to give you some of this money, but I want you to have it all, thank you so much for your kind words and help, if there is any work at all that I can do around the Convent I will be so happy to do so Molly stuttered. The Reverend mother stood up to show the interview was at an end, I think my dear she said that you should put that money away until the baby comes, one more mouth won't make much difference. You will be given a different room when your holiday is over and I will find out how useful a person you are when I confer with Sister Winifred who is in charge of chores. I want you to do something for me in return, the Mother actually smiled at Molly, anything at all an overcome Molly whispered. You must go out for the next two weeks with your friend and enjoy yourself, put everything else out of your mind and you and I will have another little

68

talk then. The Reverend Mother left the room as silently as she had come. Molly shook her head in disbelief, had that just happened? not one word of condemnation, not one word about the wrath of God, nothing only kindness, and the Sky didn't fall. she was overwhelmed and for the first time since the fateful night in Meehan's hayshed she actually felt alive again.

Chapter Seven

It was a different Molly that met Mary in the garden some time later. She had carefully put the money away in her case deciding what to do with it would be for another day. Today she was going to do as the Reverend mother had requested and enjoy herself with Mary. The said Mary could hardly believe the change in her friend as they excitedly got ready for the trip to Windsor Castle. Sister Bernadette was as good as her word and had written out a fine itinerary for the next couple of weeks. There was a bus stop right outside the Convent gate, all they had to do was get on and let the holiday begin.

The girls would remember the holiday for the test of their lives, they did all the sights, they got to London, saw big Ben, the Tower of London and Buckingham Palace, had a million other mad moments of laughter and gaiety as if they hadn't a care in the World. They went out to Brighton, they went to South End and paddled in the sea, they had so many carefree memories from that wonderful holiday but It was coming up to the last day and the dreaded thought of Molly's never going home trickled into their heads as they planned an outing to Henley. They had rang the surgery after the first week to let everyone know that they were fine but what was going to happen next had been put out of their heads. Molly was adamant that Mary was going home and Mary was just as adamant that she wasn't. What are you going to tell your parents

Molly yelled at Mary that last day, What are you going to tell yours Mary yelled back. I am going to say that I am considering a life of holiness and prayer and am going to stay in the Convent for a while and meditate Molly shouted as Mary collapsed on the bed laughing, the tears running down her face, Molly suddenly saw the funny side of her remark and collapsed laughing on top of her friend. Well said Molly reasonably when the laughter had ceased, we both can't be suddenly overcome with Saintliness, you have to go back. The matter was suddenly taken out of their hands as on the third of September, the day before their supposed departure, Neville Chamberlain announced that Great Britain declared war on Germany. They were stuck, they had a cast iron excuse, they couldn't travel.

Sister Bernadette rang her uncle, Molly's Father, and quietly told him of the dangers that the girls might face travelling, she told him that they would be safe in the Convent in the interim and even if they couldn't call on the telephone she would make sure that they wrote home. The post may be delayed with all the goings on here but I will make sure that they keep in touch. Doctor Mc Gee thanked his niece sincerely even though his heart was sore at the thought of the girls being stuck in a war situation that was nothing to do with them, he promised to tell Paddy and Annie Quinn as soon as his niece put down the phone. The Quinn's were having their dinner when the doctor pulled up outside the kitchen window. Annie immediately jumped to her feet throwing off her apron as she ran to the door, something has happened to the girls she cried grabbing

71

him by the arm. No my dear Annie, they are safe its just that they Won't be coming home yet, Hopefully the war Won't continue for long, they are secure where they are and have promised to write. In the meantime if I get anymore news I will let you know immediately. Sit down agrath and have a cup of tea Annie fussed around the doctor as she processed the news that her beloved daughter would not be coming home tomorrow as planned. The Quinn men father and son each took the news in their own way, Paddy was undone that his Red haired Mary was caught up in the war, he knew she could be in worse places than the convent but that didn't make it any easier. Pat was lost in his own world as he thought of his mad, funny laughing sister and he couldn't even put into thoughts what he felt about Molly. Maybe she would get over him he thought picturing her trusting face looking up at him. He would never forgive himself for that night in the hayshed and he knew that even if Molly forgot him he would never forget her.

The two girls were undecided as to how this new predicament would affect them, it was great to be able to stay but even if the war had provided them with the perfect excuse it wasn't something they would have chosen to be part of. Molly was already fixed up to stay in the Convent, but Mary knew that she would have to find work somehow, to support herself and also to stop herself from thinking of home and her parents. She couldn't wait to get away and now she couldn't wait to get back, but being the resilient person that she was, she resolved to make the most of this opportunity to live somewhere other than Dufflin. Molly had already spoken with Sister Winifred and she was going to be helping out in the nursery school. Next week she was going to be moved to one of the cell's that the Nun's used for sleeping in and would be able to share the meals at the school. Molly and herself would have to figure out a way to keep in touch as Mary couldn't stay in the Convent indefinitely. Mother Agnes had called Mary into the parlour and told her of a very nice Irish lady from Galway who had a boarding house around the corner, she just takes in Irish girls and you will be quite safe there, she also has knowledge of all jobs going in this area, here is her address, yourself and Molly can go around there this afternoon. I am sorry that we cannot keep you here but it would be against our rules to keep girls here who are not part of our working community. As Molly is now officially a member of our teaching staff she can stay while she decides what to do with her life. Mary thanked the Mother Superior and told her she would be fine.

The months quickly passed and the two girls felt as if they had never been anywhere else, home was not forgotten but had already become a distant memory, they had written of course but didn't know if the letters had arrived as they had heard nothing from there yet. Blackouts at night became familiar, sirens going off at all hours running to air raid shelters part of the normal. Food was rationed and long queues outside grocers' shops also became normal. Mary was now working in a munitions factory in the Industrial Estate near St. Bernard's. She was well and happy and comfortable in

Mrs Lydon's boarding House. Molly was as happy as she could be considering her circumstances. She loved working with the children and knew now that she would never give up her child for adoption, she also knew that if she kept him or her she would never be able to go back. She had tried so hard to put Pat Quinn out of her head but it just wasn't possible. His green eyes came to look into hers as she was falling asleep, his arms were around her in her dreams. She was getting near the end of her pregnancy and had been to classes for expectant mothers. The Sisters were all very protective of her and Molly knew how lucky she was to be there. Mary called twice a week and lately was full of talk about this wonderful Englishman that she had met at work. He was tall, he was handsome, he was so wonderful, that Molly almost felt that he had to be too good to be true. When am I going to meet this paragon she asked one Wednesday evening as she lowered herself awkwardly into the chair. Well Mary said next Friday is St. Patrick's day and Mrs Lydon said we'd have Green buns with Shamrocks on and that I could have George over for tea, you could come too.Its right beside you and you wouldn't have far to walk. Molly thought about how long it had been since she had been outside the Convent gate and how nice it would be to have a conversation with someone who was not a Nun or a child. I d love that she said brightening up, I can bring her the princely present of a head of lettuce and spring onions from the Convent garden.

It was a merry party that ended up in the boarding house. Mrs Lydon was as good as her word and had made the shamrock buns, she had queued for an hour to get a scrag end of ham and some bread, together with the lettuce and onions they had a feast. Molly reckoned George was everything Mary had proclaimed him to be and she was happy for her friend. Mrs Lydon produced a bottle of port wine that she had hidden in the cupboard and everyone toasted St. Patrick including George who had never even heard of him.Who is this bloke that we are toasting he asked, Mary laughed at him, he is the Patron Saint of Ireland he came over from Wales, banished all the snakes, took up a Shamrock which has three leaves, and explained to us about the three divine persons who are God being like the three leaves on one stem. He gave us our Catholic religion, George paused, wait a minute he said we are toasting some Welsh bloke who went over to Ireland and you made him a Saint, Are you all mad over there he asked Mrs Lydon who was feeling quite patriotic at this stage and had started to sing Danny boy. Molly 's heart stopped as she heard the haunting words of the song that she had danced the last dance of the rest of her life in Pat Quinn's arms, she was feeling a bit sick from the Port wine even though she had only sipped at it, she had a bad pain in her lower back and wished she could go back to her bed, she stood up to say so, when suddenly a gush of water fell from between her legs and she sat back down with a bang on the chair. Mary gaped at the floor in shock, what happened, are you all right she sat down beside her friend taking her hand which was trembling. Mrs Lydon took in the situation in a glance and sobered up quickly as Molly gave a cry of pain. Holy Saint Patrick she shouted this baby is coming and fast, get the Kettle on George, Mary run up to my room and get some sheets from the cupboard. Everyone sprung into action as Molly moaned and groaned intermittently. I have to get back to the Convent she gasped Sister Evangelina is a midwife and she is going to deliver the baby. She isn't going to deliver this child my dear said Mrs Lydon pushing up her sleeves, you are in safe hands, don't worry I have been in this situation before. Young Patrick Mc Gee made his entrance to the world on the floor of Lydon's Boarding house, screaming blue murder as the landlady took him to clean him up before handing him over to his mother. You are a fine little man she crooned, look at the red head on you, sure you'd nearly need a comb to get through those curls. Mary looked at Molly in shock as Mrs Lydon handed him over and they both new without a doubt that Patrick Mc Gee would grow up the spitting image of his father Pat Quinn. He was called Patrick, not because his father and grandfather before him bore that name but because of the Saint on whose Feast day he was born in a boarding house in England and the sky didn't fall.

Chapter Eight

The whole community in St Bernard's considered Patrick to be their child. He was such a sunny happy little boy that they all loved him. Molly never had to ask for help because somebody always provided whatever Patrick needed, He grew strong and his first steps were taken out in the garden with old gardener Willie who loved the little lad and who was to teach him many things. His hair had indeed grown auburn and curly like his fathers and his eyes were as green as emeralds. How could Molly ever forget Pat Quinn when his little double was in her arms day and night. Mary had become engaged to George Hill and they were getting married soon. Mary had asked Molly to be her bridesmaid and George was to have his best friend Charles Fuller as Best man, they were getting married in a registry office and it was to be another of the many secrets in their lives as George was not a Catholic. Maybe you will fall in love with Charles and we can be like those couples that go out together when this stupid war is over Mary said to Molly one day in the Convent as they were having fittings of their wedding finery with Sister Winifred who was a dab hand with the sewing machine. Sister had found a roll of material in the sewing room, a roll from some long time past, it was a dubious mixture of Orange and grey tweed, but Mary said it would be grand. George wouldn't care what she wore as long as she said yes and it was so long since either of the girls had any new clothes that they were as happy as could be. Sister

Winifred was as good as her word and made a lovely two piece skirt and jacket for Mary, while Molly's bridesmaid outfit was a nice slim fitting dress. They couldn't have been happier with the outcome and Mary ran over to the elderly Sister Winnifred and hugged her tightly, you are a marvel Sister she said as she jumped up and down with excitement. The Nun smiled and prayed to God that these two young girls would stay happy and well, she knew that Mary's husband to be was not a Catholic, but he seemed like a nice enough man. She hoped that Mary's parents would welcome him when they finally got through this war. She also prayed for Molly and her beautiful little boy, but also knew that the chances of any man marrying her were very slim indeed, no man would want damaged goods or to bring up another man's child. All of these thoughts Sister Winifred kept to herself as she put away her sewing machine.

The wedding took place as planned and the picture was taken by the registrar as little Patrick slept in his pushchair close by. It was sent to Annie and Paddy Quinn with not a word about religion or a sleeping grandchild in the background but filed quietly and secretly away in the minds of Mary and Molly.

The war went on and on, most houses had their own dug out or air raid shelter where families gathered as soon as the sirens went off. Food was still rationed, but children could have orange juice and milk for free, little Patrick thrived. Willie the gardener had passed away from old age and Molly and her little boy now lived in his cottage which was within the Convent grounds. She would be forever grateful to the nuns who had provided such solace and comfort to her in her darkest days. She paid a minimal rent for the cottage, no longer worked for the nursery school but was training to be a nurse in the local Hospital. She loved the training and was eager to pass her exams and be a fully fledged member of the Hospital Staff. She met Mary one Friday evening in December just before Christmas at the Odeon Cinema, they were going to see the longest film of the time ever made. It was three hours and forty two minutes long. Clark Gable and Vivian Leigh together with Thomas Mitchell were the stars of "Gone With The Wind ". Mary and Molly were so looking forward to this light relief in the middle of the madness of the British war. I hope those blinking sirens don't go off before the end of it Mary sighed to her friend. Well let's hope not, said Molly I haven't been anywhere except work or more work and study for ages. Mary felt guilty that they hadn't met up more often. She knew that Molly often struggled with looking after Patrick and keeping up with her studies and work and that she should be more of a support for her friend. Lets make a pact that we meet at least once a week from now on, It can be at the weekend when I am off or when you are free, we could bring Patrick with us where ever we go or we can get George to baby sit him if there is another film on that we want to see. Molly wasn't too sure about the baby sitting, she only ever left Patrick with Sister Bernadette or one of the other nuns who had all been unstinting with their time. That would be nice she said wistfully, but I want to get my finals out of the way before I do any gallivanting. Mary hugged her best friend, well we will go at your discretion she smiled. They were at the top of the queue for the film and as they went into the darkened cinema each of them thought of the local Cinema at home in the nearest Town of Carrickmor. They had only been once to see a cowboy film with Roy Rodgers and his horse trigger starring, which was the only offering at the time. They were lost in their thoughts during the long film, they were Scarlett O Hara, they were poor Melanie, they were caught up in the romance of Rhett Butler and him not'' giving a damn ''when suddenly the lights went off and the siren went, They ran for the door laughing, now they would never know how Rhett and Scarlett got on or if Ashley ever loved Scarlett and dumped Melanie. The throng moved fast and the girls decided to go for the Nearest shelter, most of the cinema goers also went down the stairs to the tube station. It was cold and dank but people were friendly in the circumstances as they huddled together until the all clear went. Letters came from home, they were intermittent and two could arrive at the same time. Ireland was a veritable land of milk and honey compared to Great Britain, Annie and Paddy Quinn worried about their beloved daughter and if they would ever see her again, then the news arrived that she was getting married and it nearly broke Annie's heart. Not the fact that she had found her true love, even if he was English but that she wasn't married in the Church of the Immaculate Conception in Kilmacaden, or that her father wasn't there to give her away. That the reception was far away in England instead of the homestead at Dufflin. Annie would have put on a fine spread and all the neighbours would have come to see the lovely bride. The black and white photograph arrived and was framed by Paddy and hung in the parlour. Molly's mother had by now given up on Kilmacaden and gone back to her own people in Dublin. The doctor still lived in the village but went to Dublin as often as time would allow, he knew his wife would never come back as she had never taken to "the country people". He would have gone straight away to live in Dublin too but he kept hoping that the war would soon be over and that Molly would come back to the only home she had ever known.

Patrick was now 3 years old and he, Molly and a very pregnant Mary were walking in Burnham woods, Molly had a whole week off as she had been on nights and Mary had to give up work the previous week due to her not fitting at her work bench anymore. Is this child ever going to come out she wailed to Molly, I am as big as an elephant and he should have been here two weeks ago, I am so sorry that I didn't have more sympathy for you when you were in this state. Molly laughed at her friend, once he or she arrives you will forget everything except the bundle in your arms. I know its going to be a big lumbering boy, look at the size of me, Mary replied, I will never fit into any of my clothes again. Please sit down here on this bench as I can't walk another inch. They sat in the sun and watched as Patrick gathered pine cones, do you think we will ever get back home Mary said thinking of her mother and how she would love to have her there beside her. Of course you will said Molly but you and I both know that I never will, she said sadly. Her feelings for Pat Quinn were the same as they were on the day she left but now her little boy was her sole priority he would be the only man in her life. I hope your baby does come soon she said, please let it be while I am off. Mary looked at her as she pulled herself up from the bench, well if it doesn't come before this week is up I will be making medical history.

George called for Molly the Following night at two a.m. I think the baby is coming he said can you come quickly. Molly changed into her uniform, she was now a qualified midwife, she bundled Patrick into a blanket and put him into the back of Georges car. They were only a five minute drive away and Mary could be heard shouting as they went in the front door. George, put Patrick on the sofa in the front room, he is still asleep and I will go and attend to Madam, Molly stated. George was glad to be no longer in charge, he couldn't bear to see Mary in such agony and vowed there and then that this would be their first and last child.

The agony went on until seven thirty the next morning and Patrick was stirring on the sitting room sofa. Just bring him to the bathroom and then give him some toast Molly instructed, we are almost finished having this baby, George gladly left the room, he knew the baby was almost there as Molly had told him Mary was fully dilated, he wasn't sure what she meant but he took her word for it that things were ok. He went down to Patrick and took him in his arms, he was very fond of the child and Mary was mad about him, Molly after much persuading had allowed Mary to tell George who Patrick really was. He was stunned to say the least and for the life of him couldn't understand what the problem was. The boy was born out of wedlock, but maybe Pat Quinn would love to have him and his mother in his life. He would never understand these mad Irish people and their attitude to what were in his mind very simple solvable problems.

Suddenly the sound of a baby crying startled both George and Patrick as he fed the little boy his toast, Oh my goodness he said Aunty Mary has a new little baby, lets go up and meet him, you will soon have a cousin to play with, Patrick looked at him with his big green eyes, I am not a baby he said, but I will play with him. George lifted him up on his shoulders and they bounded up the stairs. Can we come in to meet him he asked at the bedroom door. Molly laughed as she took her son from George. Of course you can, Mary doesn't always get things right you know, its not a him, it's a her, meet your beautiful daughter she grinned as she looked over at Mary who was cradling the new born with the look of a new mother staring in awe at the most beautiful child in the world.

Everything settled down to normal. Mary and George named their daughter Catherine and one Sunny day in Windsor they took her to St. Bernard's Convent where the Chaplain Father Horton Baptised her. Molly was her God mother and her only God parent. Catherine was soon shortened to Kate who with her blonde curls and blue eyes looked like an angel. Patrick was very protective of his little cousin and let her play with his toys whenever they met up while Kate adored her older cousin and cried when they were separated. Mary and Molly agreed that they were the best looking children in England. George got promoted in the munitions factory and himself and his small family were as contented as people could be in this war. Then one June day in 1945 it was over. The war was over, people were going around kissing each other and grinning like idiots. It was such a relief to tear down the blackouts, to be able to buy food that wasn't rationed any more. Air raid shelters were used to grow mushrooms in or to keep the garden tools, nobody missed the sirens and suddenly the World seemed a wonderful place. Mary knew that now the war was over her parents would be expecting a visit from them, Maybe not just yet as Kate was still only two but soon and she didn't know how she would be prepared or that.Her parents didn't know that George wasn't a Catholic, they knew he was English but that was as far as it went. Doctor Mc Gee was still waiting in Kilmacaden for Molly to come back. He rang the Convent and asked for a message to be left for her to ring him soon.

The friends were in Mary's house as the children played with wooden bricks on the floor, Patrick was building a wall while Kate knocked it down every time he got it to a certain height, he good naturedly let her as she dimpled her smile at him. What on earth am I going to say to my father she wailed to Mary, He is going to want me home, what am I going to do. Well said Mary slowly

84

you could leave Patrick with us and go and visit him, you know he would be happy here. I do know that Molly agreed but I can't go back I just can't. Mary knew without it being said that the reason was her brother and she didn't know what to do either. Tell him that you are still studying and that as soon as you are qualified you will try and get home. That would be a lie said the fully qualified Molly, I can't tell him a lie, well tell him you are going to do more studying and then go and study something, Mary grinned at her friend. You should start studying mankind and get yourself a nice husband and Patrick a daddy, he was asking me the other day if George could be his dad. She took one look at Molly's stricken face and wished she had kept her mouth shut. Oh Molly I am sorry, I shouldn't have said anything. Molly straightened herself while tears prickled behind her eyes, Are you not over my brother yet Mary asked her quietly as the children played at their feet. Mary, I will say this once to you and only once I will love Pat Quinn until the day I die and as much as I regret that night in the hayshed, I can never regret my Darling boy. She swept up the little boy in her arms, this is my man my only man. Five year old Patrick disentangled himself from her arms, Mummy please put me down, she is always doing this Auntie Mary he groaned, Mary laughingly ruffled his auburn curls, that's because she loves you she said, as two year old Kate not to be outdone in the cuddling came toddling over to Molly, luv me luv me she lisped. Of course I love you too my little cherub Molly sang as she shot Mary a look that said, this conversation is over.

Patrick had started school in St. Bernard's that September and Kate went to nursery school also at St. Bernard's. Mary had written to her mother every week since the war had ended, she kept using Kate being too young, or George's work as an excuse not to travel over to Ireland. Meanwhile several years passed and Paddy and Annie Quinn's grandchildren grew up well and strong with beautifully polished English accents. The transfer for George knocked the stuffing out of both Mary and Molly's lives. Mary, because she knew she would have to introduce her Protestant husband to her family and the narrow minded world that was Dufflin and Kilmacaden Molly's because her best friends and her god daughter would be lost to her. She couldn't think straight, she knew Patrick's world would also be a very different place without his Aunt, uncle and cousin, she also knew she couldn't say anything to mar this great achievement and step up for George. She put on a brave face as she congratulated them on their new life. The two friends met up for afternoon tea at The Buckingham Arms where Mary's wedding meal had taken place all those years ago. I am so sorry, Mary wept as the tears fell unchecked down her face, I wish to God none of this had happened, George is determined to take this promotion and there is nothing I can do. Kate, who by now was also attending St. Bernard's and had made lots of friends was at seven no less cute than she had been as a baby, I have to uproot her from everything she's ever known and take her to the back of beyond and I have to leave you my very best friend in the whole World and my Patrick too she

86

sobbed, Molly who was also dropping a tear or two tried to be the stronger person. It's not the back of beyond, its home for Heaven's sake if you only knew how much I wish I could pack up and go back home you wouldn't be whinging so much she hiccupped as she tried to comfort her friend. It worked, as Mary looked at Molly and thought how selfish she was being, she was going home, she would get to see her parents and her brother while poor Molly was stuck in England for ever. oh how selfish I am she gulped, when I should be happy that I have a choice. We will write to each other every week and maybe I will get back on holidays in a while after we are settled. Where we are going is a good bit away from Kilmacadan and maybe you would chance coming over with Patrick for a week or two. Maybe smiled Molly, who had no intention of ever taking that trip, sure it will be great, we can also talk sometimes on the telephone. They felt marginally better as they drank their tea and pretended to be ladies of leisure as the Buckinghamshire sun sank in the sky.

Chapter Nine

Mary heard her Father tell George about the price of cattle and how the war had affected Ireland as they ate the fine tea that Annie had prepared. Kate was very quiet and sat between her mother and father listening to the voices flow over her head. Would you like to meet Ginger the cat her uncle Pat asked her nodding towards the kitchen, yes please she said looking to her mother for permission to get down from the table, go on Mary smiled, be gentle and he won't scratch you, Ginger who was nearly too lazy to scratch himself, never mind Kate, was curled up at the fire and was only too delighted to have someone to rub him and ruffle his fur. I love him already Uncle Pat she said looking out under her blonde curly fringe, I wish I could bring him home with me. Well now said Pat isn't that a strange coincidence, the Collins's next to us have a fine big mammy cat and isn't she after having kittens, they are looking for homes for them, maybe your mammy and daddy will let you have one said Pat as he hunkered down beside his niece, she jumped up and threw her arms around him knocking him onto the floor beside Ginger in the process, Mummy she yelled as Mary came flying into the kitchen, she saw Pat on the floor beside the cat as Kate hung onto him for dear life, what in heavens name is going on her she said as Kate scrambled to her feet leaving Pat grinning up at her from the floor looking very much like the Pat who used to pull her pigtails when she was Kate's age, What have you done she said looking at Pat, He hasn't done anything mummy squealed Kate trying to pull her uncle up from the mat at the fire, he has just told me something very exciting. Mary looked from one to the other in bewilderment, well she said what is this wonderful news. Kate looked up at her mother her blue eyes shining, please mummy please say yes she begged. How can I say yes when I don't know what you are talking about Mary, gave Pat a look that wasn't very promising, By now George had also come into the kitchen to see what all the racket was and Kate knew she now had a better chance than ever, she ran over to her father, catching him around the knees please say yes daddy please, Annie and Paddy were also in the kitchen at this stage and as the little girl was almost incoherent with delight Pat thought he had better get the news out himself. Collins's next door have new kittens and they are looking for homes for them I thought Kate here might be able to take one off their hands he said, of course Mummy and daddy have to be ok about it he said to his niece. Mary was looking at him with a look that could kill, you might have asked us first she muttered. How on earth will we pack a kitten in with everything else that's in the car. But can I have one please gulped Kate, I will love him and look after him and everything she stammered. Mary knew she was beaten when George replied well if we are getting this kitten you will have to. When can I get the kitten was the next question followed by an answer from Mary, seeing as how your uncle Pat was so good as to tell you about the kitten maybe he will bring you over to

Collins's farm tomorrow to pick it. Once again Pat found himself manhandled by the surprisingly strong delicate looking Kate. Oh you will bring me won't you she screeched holding him around the knees. Well It seems I don't have much choice he said smiling at his niece, when I have the milking done in the morning and you have gathered the eggs we will go over there. Yes, yes shouted Kate who had suddenly become transformed into a very happy little girl, Her grandparents smiled at her enthusiasm I love this farm and tomorrow I am going to collect eggs and then my kitten. Thank you everybody. They all laughed as Paddy and Pat prepared to go out to the farmyard to finish the days work. Why don't you take Kate for a walk around the yard and see if you can find all the places where the eggs are Mary asked George, handing him a basket, Granny didn't collect them today so that you could do it. You will find them all before dark. She badly needed to get her mother on her own to tell her about the protestant George. Come on daddy the little girl squealed let's go and find eggs.

Mary followed her mother into the back kitchen where the famous new water tap stool proudly like a sentinel over the sink. Mam I need to talk to you about something Molly said nervously, lets go into the kitchen and have another cup of tea. Annie looked at her daughter's serious face, is there something wrong a chara she asked as Mary sat down with a plonk at the scrubbed kitchen table. Well It depends said Mary not really knowing where to start, You know that George and I are Married, she began as her mother looked at her in bewilderment, Yes, she said sure I have the lovely picture of it in the parlour, well we are married said a white faced Mary but we didn't get married in a Church. There she had said it and her mother hadn't passed out from shock and the sky didn't fall, but looking at her mam's face Mary knew shock was setting in, you didn't get married in a Church she whispered and it was almost as if the Parish Priest and all of the neighbours were listening in the next room, Why, Mary was it the war ? no mam it was because George is not a Catholic, he is Church of England, Now, Annie sat down with a plonk and her face was as white as her daughters. He is not a Catholic she kept saying to herself, but what about Kate, what about my granddaughter she muttered looking at Mary as if she had never seen her before. Kate is a Catholic she was baptised and she will soon be making her First Holy Communion and Mam, George is a good man he loves me and Kate and he is very good to us. Lord save us what will your father say, what will Father Murphy say, what will the neighbours say, Annie gasped. Mam I do care about what dad thinks but I don't care what Father Murphy or the neighbours think, they are not married to George, I am, and I am very happy, will you please tell dad all of this, I can't go through it twice. Annie sat in the chair thinking of how she had so wished that Mary had got married in their Parish Church and now she was thanking her God that they didn't. What would Paddy make of it all, what would the neighbours say. They did have a protestant family living in the village of Kimacredan, the Tinsons, Bert Tinson, his wife Dorothy and their two sons. The

91

sons were away at boarding school and Bert and his wife lived quietly nodding at the neighbours when they met them, but the likelihood of any of the sons getting married to any of the local Catholic girls was as remote a possibility as Annie losing her faith. Where did you get married, are you sure you are married, she quizzed her daughter as Mary tried to fill her in. We are of course married only it was in a registry office and it is legal and binding. But its not legal in the eyes of the Catholic Church Annie stated the obvious to Mary whose heart was breaking at her mother's reaction to the news. We will have to tell Father Murphy and maybe he will marry you and George on the quiet. Mary was horrified, she wished they had never come home and then she told herself off at the thought of never seeing her parents and brother again. What was she going to tell George, How was Paddy Quinn going to take the news. Her mother got up from the table and walked up and down the kitchen as if she was training for a race. She took her apron off and frightened Mary by the determined look on her face. That's it she said when we tell your father, we will talk to His reverence in the Parochial house, but it will have to be when the housekeeper is out because she is so nosey she will tell everyone. You and George will have to come down again next weekend if we can arrange the marriage for then. Mary was speechless at this plan of her mothers, she opened her mouth in protest but the chattering of Kate could be heard coming into the house with George's voice answering, Granny, look at all the eggs we found she shouted, do you think we got them all. Annie pulled herself together. Well aren't you the clever little girl she smiled, Mary noticed that she didn't look at George. It was getting dark outside at this stage and the Quinns, Father and son came into the back kitchen. Annie was shepherding them all back into the parlour where the fire was roaring up the chimney and the damp had all but gone from the room, Isn't this nice she said looking daggers at Mary, it's a pity that you can't stay for the weekend instead of going back tomorrow, why don't you come back next weekend for the few days. Kate who was all ears jumped up Oh please Mummy lets come back again, I love it here said the excited little girl, well I don't know pet said Mary thinking how she never knew how devious her mother was, daddy may have something else to do. George looked up, its fine he said, I still have lots of petrol in the car and it would be a good chance to collect the kitten next week when we have prepared somewhere for it to sleep. Kate's face fell but she knew her daddy was right they really needed to get ready for the kitten, well ok she said but I can still go over there tomorrow and pick one out she pleaded looking at her uncle Pat. Of course you can said Pat and I will get a box from the Creamery when I am down there with the milk, I will put some straw in it and you can have it on the seat beside you on the way home next weekend. Mary was trapped and there was nothing she could do, Poor George who was totally unaware of the drama being played was happy to bring his family back to the farm next weekend and to these lovely people who were his in-laws.

Paddy Quinn scratched his head and frowned as he pondered over this latest news of Mary and the ''protestant '' as Annie was now referring to George as, He was as shocked at the news as Annie but had a much more forgiving attitude, sure Mary didn't pick who she was going to fall in love with he said to his wife who was still pacing up and down while the rest of the family had gone to bed, He seems like a very nice man and Mary is very happy, and she is not the first Catholic to marry a protestant, but stuttered Annie they are not married in the eyes of the Church and we have to get Father Murphy to marry them as quickly as we can and not have them living in sin. Paddy thought this was going a bit far and he said so, although he knew in his heart and soul that Annie was right. What does George think of this second time marriage he asked his wife as he tried to keep her in his vision as she paced up and down, Mary will be telling him now, I'm sure she said. Well said paddy we Won't solve anything tonight so lets go to bed and tomorrow while Pat brings the young one to look at the kittens, we will go up to Father Murphy before he does the early confessions. Annie had to be satisfied at that as Paddy took out his beads to say the nightly rosary that they both said before they turned in for the night.

Upstairs Mary was trying to explain to George how her mother felt about the marriage, she doesn't think we are properly tied at all she said to her once again bewildered husband. We have to go to the priest tomorrow to arrange a proper marriage and Blessing she whispered quietly as Kate was sleeping in the settle bed beside them. I will never understand the half of this stuff that goes on between you and your Church he whispered back but I don't mind marrying you again sweet heart. Let's just make your lovely parents happy. Mary hadn't the heart to tell him that at least one of her parents wasn't happy and she dreaded to think what Father Murphy was going to say. He would probably say she was the one to blame, she was the one to look outside her own kind, she just knew he would blame her.

The sun was shining the next day as Kate and Pat got ready to head over to Collins's, why don't you come with us he said to Mary, you could talk to Jim Collins about old times, he is married now to Kitty O' Dowd, she is from the Gaeltacht in Connemara and they have two grand boys, indeed and she won't said Annie quickly, butting in before Mary got a chance to answer, we have a bit of business to attend to, yourself and Kate can stay for an hour or two over there. Pat knew by his mother's tone of voice that this was an order and that something was up, he looked at his sister who shook her head said, I will see them another day but Kate and yourself can take your time choosing the kitten. Right so he said We'll see you later as he took his excited niece by the hand. Bye bye mummy and daddy she dimpled as they left from the back door.

It was a very silent quartet that sat in the back of the Church waiting for Father Murphy, Paddy had gone to the Parochial House to ask the housekeeper where he was, while the other three had waited in the car.

George knew something had shifted in his welcoming relationship with Annie to mistrust, He knew he hadn't done anything wrong but she made him feel that he had. Father Murphy was already in the Church preparing for early Confessions Paddy informed them as he came back, Do you think maybe we should wait in the car Annie and let these pair go in on their own. Annie shook her head vigorously indeed and we won't sit in the car we are all going in she said as she got out with a determined look on her face, They shuffled awkwardly into the back of the Church where Father Murphy was sorting candles, he looked at them in surprise, Well now he said and to what do I owe this visit. Annie immediately jumped in, well Father, it's a very delicate matter and we need your help to sort it out. Well now did what did yourself and Paddy do that warrants this help he said looking from one to the other. Indeed Father tis not us at all she said but this young couple here. Father murphy looked at Mary's white face, he had Baptised her, given her First Communion and he was present when she received her Confirmation, what is it my child he said taking in the handsome blonde man who put his arm protectively around Mary. Annie butted in again before Mary got a chance. Her husband, Father is not a Catholic and they were married in a Registry office, you must marry them Father to make it legal in the eyes of the Church. Father Murphy took in the situation and the state of Mary, who stood between her husband and her father like a condemned woman. Annie and Paddy he said why don't you wait outside while I have a word with this young couple. Paddy stood up at once and pulled the reluctant Annie towards the door, we will so Father he said as he practically manhandled his wife outside. Come into the Sacristy where we won't be disturbed the Priest motioned to Mary and George. They traipsed into the Room at the back of the Altar while Mary tried to quell the sick feeling in her stomach. Sit down he said and tell me your story. Mary looked at George who spoke with his cultured English accent. We met at my work place Reverend, Father Murphy gave a slight smile but didn't correct him, I knew that this lovely Irish girl was the only one I ever wanted to Marry, she did put up a lot of protestations at the time, mainly her religion, my religion, her parents wishing her to marry a good Irishman, but I wore her down, if there is to be any blame let it be mine. Father Murphy instantly liked this sincere young man and thought of the many louts around that Mary might have chosen had she stayed at home, He thought of the women he saw at Mass with bruises on their faces where they "had fallen" or the many wives he had to bury because the fifteenth or sixteenth child was the undoing of them and he knew that this man in front of him would be a good husband. I will tell you a story he said that none of my flock know and that I would like you to keep to yourselves, it's not that I am ashamed of my story but that I think its just my business and belongs to nobody else. Mary who was feeling a bit more relaxed looked at the priest in surprise. My father was Jimmy Murphy from Co. Donegal, He lived on the republican side of Ireland in a small town called Pettigo, one day he went to a cattle fair in Irvinstown and was involved in an accident with a bull. He was brought to hospital in Enniskillen where his injuries while not life threatening kept him in hospital for several weeks. While he was there he was looked after by a nurse by the name of Ivy Windham, he knew like yourself George as soon as he saw her that this was the girl that he wanted to spend the rest of his life with and he knew by the way she looked at him that she knew it too. He told her before he left the hospital that he was going to marry her. All of this is leading to the fact that my mother was a protestant and my Father was a Catholic. Both of their families were horrified and tried to make them see sense. They threatened them with expulsion from their homes, their kith and kin. It didn't deter them in fact it made them stronger They went to Belfast where nobody knew them, they had the Banns read as you had to do in those days and they got Married in the Catholic Church, my mother had to promise to rear any children of the marriage as Catholics, which she did, there was myself and my two sisters and she made us say our prayers and receive the Sacraments, indeed it was she and not my father who was the one who kept us in our religion. We never got to meet any of our grandparents or other relatives. When I got the calling to enter the priesthood, my mother was overwhelmed and I firmly believe that only for her I would not be sitting here in the Sacristy of my Church. I am happy to say that before she died she had converted to Catholicism. Now my children, If you are here at 8am on next Saturday morning I will gladly officiate at your marriage, I will bring My Curate, Fr. Mc

Gowan with me and Mary you bring your Brother Pat and they can be your witnesses. There is no need for anyone else to know our business. The priest stood up as Mary and George thanked him. We will be here Father she said, the first words she had spoken since they had entered the room. The relief showed in her face and she totally revised her opinion of Father Murphy. George shook his hand and smiled, even my mother-in-law can't fault this plan Reverend he said as he exchanged looks with the priest, who also permitted himself a slight grin.

Chapter Ten

It was with a light heart that Mary told her mother of the plans for next Saturday, Annie wasn't happy that herself and Paddy couldn't be there, but knew that the less people that were around the Church the less suspicious it would look and to keep things quiet she just nodded. George pulled in on the Street just as Pat and Kate came around the corner from Collins's. She could hardly contain herself. The cat has four kittens three of them are ginger and one is black. I picked the black one he is like a ball of fur and I am going to call him sooty, because he is as black as soot. I can't wait for next weekend when we are going to take him home. Mary wanted to get Pat to one side to ask him to be their Marriage witness on the following weekend, so she told George and Kate to gather the eggs once again, the hens will have laid more nice brown eggs so be a good girl and collect them for granny, Kate didn't need to be told twice as she tore into the back kitchen to get the egg basket.

Mary took her brother by the arm, come with me up as far as the top field she said I haven't been up there for so long He looked at her in surprise but just nodded his head, come on so he said I will let the cows out later. They walked the track that they had so often raced up to the top field when they were younger. She told him all, the marriage in the registry office, their mother's horror and the official marriage on Saturday, she didn't mention Father Murphy's secret, that would remain his

100

secret. Pat took it all in, you have done and seen so much more in your life than I have, he said, Are you happy Mary. Mary nodded vigorously, I wouldn't change anything she said, well he said that is all that matters I will be proud to stand up beside you on Saturday. Mam is hung up on religion and you and George are very good to do this to please her. Mary interrupted him, well I will actually feel happier myself too she said. Pat looked at her and nearly knocked the stuffing out of her with, his next words, What happened to your great friend Molly Mc Gee he asked not looking at her, did you keep in touch, did she find herself a nice protestant too, he asked, holding his breath as he waited for her answer. Oh we did keep in touch Mary said not wanting to lie but choosing her words carefully in case she betrayed her friend. She is a qualified nurse and midwife and is busy studying for other exams that she is taking. We write to each other now and then. She didn't meet anybody that she wanted to marry I think she just loves her job too much. Pat slowly let out the breath he had been holding. Has she any notion of coming over home, her mother never comes from Dublin now but Doctor Mc Gee still has the house and comes occasionally. Mary said she didn't think Molly had time but that she wasn't really sure what her friends plans were. She quickly changed the subject, what about yourself she teased, how come there is no Mrs Pat Quinn yet, do you remember that awful Cissie O' Shea she was mad about you. Pat grinned, she was mad about everybody, but she knew which side her bread was buttered on and she married John Downey, remember the Solicitor of Lynch and Downey Solicitors where you were supposed to end up. They have one son John Jnr and live in Downey's old barracks of a house on Main Street. I suppose the one I want to marry isn't around here he said cryptically, Mary shrugged her shoulders, well I think you are wasted, you would make a great husband, she couldn't quite say ''and father'' as the words would have stuck in her neck. Do you still have the get away money that Dan sent you, under the bed. Pat looked at her in surprise, how did you know about that he asked, what were you doing under my bed. Mary laughed, I wasn't literally under your bed, I just knew that Dan sent the fare to America and that you never went. You are right he admitted it still is under my bed. I couldn't leave mam and dad and when you went off to England and got stuck there during the war I had to help out here. Don't get me wrong he said looking at her stricken face, I wanted to stay, I love the farm but sometimes it gets lonely with just the parents for company. You will have to come and visit us in Ballybrea, Mary replied, I will look up the all local spinsters and invite them to tea while you are there. Pat laughed, I will come surely he said but I don't want to meet the spinsters as you say, but I promised Kate that I would come to see the kitten soon. They walked back down to the farm house with no further talk of marriage or travel

The following Saturday morning saw Pat, Mary and George at Dufflin Parish Church before most of the villagers were out of their beds. The Parish Priest and the curate met them in the Sacristy where the ceremony took place. Within thirty minutes Mary Quinn and George Hill had been recognised and united by the Catholic Church in the Sacrament of Marriage. Mary was amazed at the relief that flowed through her afterwards. She could now go to Confession with her mother this evening, she hadn't realised how much it had weighed on her mind. She thought of the first wedding in the registry office in England and how much having Molly there with her meant, She was so sad for her friend at the way things had turned out and for her Brother whom she had of course forgiven for his part in it all, she knew instinctively that he would have followed Molly if he had known about the baby regardless of the Parish gossip. As they thanked Father Murphy he took her one side. You are a good woman Mary, be happy, you have a good man and that is one of the main things in a good marriage. May God Bless you my child, will I see you at Confession this evening he asked knowingly, Indeed you will Father said Mary contentedly as they walked out into the pale morning sunshine.

Pat and Kate were in Collins's hayshed where four kittens snuggled contentedly into their mother cat. Kate was a bit worried about the fact that they were taking Sooty away from her mummy. But Jim Collins explained that the other kittens were also going to different homes and that the mother cat would be glad of a rest. Kate accepted this explanation as her uncle Pat carefully put the kitten into the straw filled wooden box. She couldn't wait to get home to show off her new pet to Lily and Terence.

Chapter Eleven

It was the last week in May and the First Communion was in two weeks, Mary had bought the chosen Communion dress from Mrs Canny who was also the village dressmaker. It had to be taken up as it was a little bit long and Mary didn't want Kate to trip up on her special day. She was on her way to collect it when she bumped into Sally Sheehan heading in the same direction. I' m going over to Canny's to collect her ladyships dress she announced to Sally as they hurried up the street out of a sudden Summer shower. Me too laughed Sally Nell Canny is after making the most gorgeous outfit for Terrence in white just like he wanted. Tom Couldn't make any complaint as the support for the white outfit had come from a most unlikely source. Father Hoey himself, no less had been in the shop when Terence had ran in on his way home from school. Say hello to his reverence Tom shouted at Terence as he skidded to a halt beside the priest. Hello said Terence blushing up to the roots of his fair hair, Hello What, roared Tom, Hello Father he whispered. Father Hoey recognised him from the Communion class, Well my boy, he said are you all ready for the big day. Yes Father stuttered Terrence I have a white suit. Tom, who had put every obstacle he could think of in the way of the white suit groaned, Oh my God he thought what is Father Hoey going to think. Father Hoey looked at Terrence, Well now he said isn't that great, when I was in Rome, where the Pope lives he added for Terrence's benefit, I gave First Holy Communion to a class of Italian boys and they all wore white suits and arn't you the clever lad to be the first boy in Ballybae to be wearing one. Tom looked at the priest in astonishment, as he asked for a lollypop for the boy, his sisters who had just burst into the shop were speechless for once as Terence said thank you Father as he ran up the stairs, his sisters galloping after him and in to his Mam who couldn't for the life of her understand what all the excitement was about. Father Hoey was in the shop Mam Amy gulped, and he gave Terence a lollypop, but we didn't get any, Let him speak said Sally gently taking the pop until after dinner. What did you do she asked, I told him about my white suit, he said, Oh no, Sally groaned to herself, I bet your father loved that. Father Hoey says I am a very smart boy to be the first from Ballybrae to wear a white suit like all the Italian boys do. Sally looked at him askance, did he really say that she asked, yes he did, ask daddy Terence replied. Well thought Sally to herself there is a God after all, she couldn't wait to get down to let Tom up for his dinner and to hear his version of events.

Terence couldn't wait for his father to come up either, he usually went up to the attic to do his homework while the girls pestered Tom at his dinner, but this evening he was sitting at the table when his father came in. Well now isn't this nice said Tom taking his plate from on top of the oven, that hung from the crook over the fire where Sally had left it warming. Why did Father Hoey give Terence a pop and none for us said Amy who was always to the front of conversations, Well said Tom scratching his head, he thinks Terence is clever to have wanted a white suit for First Communion, seemingly the Italian boys where Father Hoey was before he came here always wore white. The twins beamed at Terence, you clever boy they chanted in unison, we will have the smartest brother in the Church. Terence seemed to grow in stature at all this praise and glory and he thought his father looked at him with respect. It was a great feeling and it gave the little boy a quietly growing air of confidence.

Sally and Mary arrived at Canny's to find their respective Packages waiting for them. When Sally and Terence had gone to gone to the shop some weeks previously to inspect the white trousers Terence had spotted, Mrs Canny laughed as she took it down from the hook amongst all the other items of clothing that also hung in a glorious array of dresses, skirts, caps, cardigans, pullovers in no particular order. This is a pair of football shorts she explained patiently to Terence you couldn't possibly wear these for your First Communion. The little boy's face fell, while Sally heaved a sigh of relief, that was to be short lived however, when Nell Canny, who couldn't bear Terence's look of disappointment announced, hold on a minute I have a bolt of white Bainin material here that is just about enough for a little boys suit, I could have it made up in no time It's not really long enough for anything else. Sally was beaten, she thanked Mrs Canny who was already out from behind the counter with a tape ready to measure up Terence.

The women took their respective packages each with it's precious cargo. I had a small bit left over Sally, so I'made a little dickey bow to go with the suit said Mrs Canny as they paid her and thanked her for her help. That woman is a treasure remarked Mary, indeed she is Sally answered as they made their way back down the street and she told her about the episode with Father Hoey and the white suited Italian boys. Mary laughed, I remember when I was getting Communion and my older sister sent me a package from America with the most wonderful things in it and I knew by my mother's face that she wasn't all that keen on me being so glorious looking but I twisted my father's arm and nothing to this day has ever made me feel so important and happy. I hope Terence wears his white suit with pride.

The same Terence, who a few months ago, would have been stuck on his own in a corner somewhere, was a changed boy since becoming friends with Kate and Lily Banaghan and was at that moment stroking Sooty, Kate's kitten who by now was showing signs of becoming a cat. He had known Lily all his life but had never even spoken to her before Kate came on the scene. They all adored Sooty even though Lily had several cats on the farm and also a sheep dog, but she had never made a pet of any of them. They were working animals and had to earn their keep. The cats kept the barn free from mice and rats and Shep the dog knew how to round up the sheep and bring in the cows for milking. All of the Banaghans, Lily's mother Lizzie and her brothers Seamus and Sean earned their keep since their father had died of T.B. when Lily was two. She didn't really remember him although her mother tried to keep his memory alive for her children by relating stories about how good a man he was. Lily was the pet and was minded by her brothers who took very good care of their little sister. Kate was envious of her with her two big brothers and of Terence with his three sisters while both Terence and Lily, while they loved their siblings would like to have been an only child like Kate. They were discussing the big day coming up on June tenth, the Feast of Corpus Christi. My Granny and grandad and my uncle Pat are coming up from Dufflin Kate exclaimed. Molly whose grandparents were dead long before she was born said nothing. Terence announced that he had two grandfathers and one grandmother coming for the occasion. It will be the best day ever Kate said, she was losing her English accent rapidly and now called her mother, mammy like every other Irish child. She was doing quite well at her Irish and Miss Conlon had said Maith an Cailin the other day, which Kate knew was good girl. She was learning How to dance a reel and double jig at the Irish dancing classes that took place once a week at the village hall. She still missed lots of things but it didn't bother her any more. I have to go home now Lily said my mammy wants me to collect the eggs and put the hens to bed. Can we come said Terence much to the surprise of the two girls as he seldom said much unless one of them initiated the conversation. Can I come too said Kate, I ll tell my mammy first and we can help you put in the hens and gather the eggs. Lily was delighted at the offer of help, she didn't like the hens one bit They pecked at her when she was shooing them into the hen house. Are you going to tell your mammy where we are going Kate said to Terence, no he said she'll be busy in the shop as my dad is gone to the Cash and Carry, she knows I'm with my friends. They left Sooty in his box and went through Kates back garden and by the kitchen window where Mary was washing the dishes, I'm going to Lily's house mammy she shouted, Mary smiled, she was delighted at the way Kate had settled in and the fact that she had made friends. Be back here at six O' Clock for your tea she said as she waved them off out of the gate. They collected the eggs carefully and brought them into Lizzie Banaghan who was at the tin washtub scrubbing the boys' clothes. She wiped the sweat from her forehead with a sudsy hand. That's great she said did you put the latch on in the hen house in case the fox gets them. Yes mammy we did said Lily, can we go and play in the paddock for a while, Seamus and Sean are up there playing ball. Go on off with you so Said lizzie with a smile, Please Mrs Banaghan will you shout out to me when its nearly six o'clock asked Kate, I will indeed a grath said the woman who's life was controlled by the clock. Get up at six, get the cows milked, get the breakfast at seven. Get the children off to school for nine. Feed the cattle, feed the hens, do the washing. Then from ten thirty until three O' Clock, when the children would be finished school Lizzie did all the necessary things around the farm that her late husband would normally have done. She was as good as any man at raking and making cocks of hay, she could pull a calf and knew when each cow was due to go to the bull, she could take the worm out of a hen's craw, she knew when each sheep was due to lamb, but she drew the line though at killing the pig and she got her neighbour Larry Devine, to do the deed each year, She took the salted bacon and marked out each month's share as it hung on a big crook in the back kitchen, She set potatoes, turnips cabbages and carrots, She churned the milk and made her own butter, she made Jam. She also sold the bulk of her eggs as did every other famer's wife, but while the egg money was for the most, their own spending money with Lizzie it was about all she had to spare to buy clothes and necessities for her children and while they were mostly self sufficient money was always scarce. She had put off buying Lily a first Communion dress as it would take such a big chunk out of the money she was saving to send Seamus to the secondary school next year. She knew the day was drawing near and she would have to make a decision, it was either buy the dress or go to second hand clothes shop in the nearest big town. She hated the fact that Lily would have to make do as the little girl seldom asked for anything, with the boys it was easier as Seamus didn't care what he wore and Sean always wore Seamus's hand me downs. Lizzie knew this wouldn't last much longer either. She could hear the children screaming with laughter up in the paddock and decided to go up and watch them. It was five thirty and she would go mad and spend a whole half an hour doing nothing for once until it was time for Kate to go home. As she came to the gate she saw Seamus and Kate running mad after the ball while Lily and Sean were going just as mad trying to take it from them.

Young Terence Sheehan was running up and down in the makeshift goals which were made from a stick stuck at each end to mark the spot. Seamus got the ball and tore up the paddock with the other three in hot pursuit, he took aim at the waiting Terence who dived on the ball just before it went over the line between the sticks. They all collapsed in a heap laughing as they saw Lizzie coming towards them, We are playing football sang Kate, I have never played before it is great fun, Terence also spoke up, I have never played football before either, Seamus gave him a friendly shove, well you are a mighty Goalie he told him, Mam he never let in one goal, I 've never seen the like he said to his mother. She smiled at them all. Good stuff Terence wait until your father hears about this news, you must be good if Seamus says so and she gave her son a pat on the back. Will you be our Goalie at school on Monday Sean said to the by now elated Terence, Well ok he said bashfully, do you really want me, of course we do said Sean we would have you in there long ago if we had known how good you were. I think it's time you were all going back to your homes Lizzie said, we will all walk over with Kate and then drop off Terence on the way back. This went down a treat as the Banaghan children so seldom got their mother to themselves in any form of leisure even if was only a walk. They arrived at Hills just as George was pulling up in his car from work. The two Banaghan boys were fascinated by the fact that Kate's father had a motor car. They were drawn to it like a magnet. George opened the door, good evening he saluted them with a flourish as he doffed his hat. Lizzie hadn't met him before although she knew Mary from the First Communion meetings, She liked his clipped English accent and how he now asked the boys would they like a short spin in the car if it was all right with their mother, Lizzie nodded as all three boys who by now were salivating at the mouth at the thought of a spin in the Motor car. They jumped into the back as George ushered the spellbound Lily into the front seat with Kate. Mary had by now come out to see what all the racket was about laughed at the air of excitement in the car. Come on in she said to Lizzie, we will have a cup of tea while they do the grand tour. She ushered lizzie into the nicest sitting room she had ever seen, I don't think my shoes are clean enough to go in there she remarked holding back, we have just been in the paddock and I' m afraid it's a bit mucky, Mary looked at Lizzies broken brown laced up shoes, and at her patched skirt and well worn cardigan. I didn't think we would be meeting anyone she said as Mary lead her into the kitchen instead. Sit down, its great to have you for a cup of tea, I should have had you over ages ago, you have been so kind to Kate and she absolutely adores Lily, I don't know how we would have coped if Lily hadn't taken her in hand. Lizzie swelled with pride at the praise heaped on her beloved daughter. This First Communion day is taking over everything Mary laughed, did you get the dress, Lily was saying that you were very busy but that you would be getting it soon. Mary was astounded when Lizzie suddenly burst into tears, It was the kind words, the lovely warm kitchen and the fact that the thought of the second hand dress that had opened the floodgates. I am so sorry she said rubbing her eyes with the hem of her cardigan, I don't know what came over me, Its all right said Mary gently, she knew that Lizzies husband had died when Lily was small and that Things were probably hard for the young woman in front of her. You can talk to me she said I am a good listener and I am very good at keeping secrets. Once Lizzie started she couldn't stop, It all came out, The lack of money, the hard work, the second hand Communion dress, no grandparents only dead ones, it all came pouring out like a waterfall of words. Mary put her arm around the sobbing woman, its fine she said you have come at a great time for Communion dresses. Lizzie stopped sobbing at looked at her in bewilderment, When I was a little girl, my sister sent me the most amazing dress and I had forgotten all about it, but my mother gave it to me the last time we were down there, all wrapped up in mothballs. Kate had already fallen for a dress in Cannys and we had bought it before I found out that this one was still about and in good shape, She hurried up to the bedroom where the dress was in the bottom of the wardrobe, I didn't tell Kate and she has never seen it, all it needs is a good wash to get the smell of mothballs out of it she said to Lizzie as she brought it into the kitchen. Lizzie was gobsmacked at the beautiful dress, I will pay you for it she stammered as Mary rewrapped it in brown paper. Indeed you Won't sure Kate doesn't need it she'll only be getting Communion once and you will be doing me a favour by taking it. Mary was adamant, I will tell my mother not to say a word, just leave it here and I will drop it in to you when The children are at school. That's settled she said as the kettle boiled and she took down the biscuit tin. Lizzie felt so happy that she didn't have to worry about the dress any more. Is there anything I can do to thank you, well there is one thing Mary smiled why don't you and the children join us here for breakfast after the Mass, Kate will be delighted to have her best friend here and to show her off to her grandparents and her uncle Pat. We have lots of space and it will be no bother. Lizzie was overwhelmed, I have to do something, please let me bring something I can do homemade butter, jam and brown bread she pleaded, That will be perfect smiled Mary, my bread still leaves a lot to be desired, brown bread and your homemade butter and jam will be wonderful and by the time the tour of the village in George's car was over and the excited children arrived back Lizzie's tearful face had disappeared and everything was back to normal. The Boys were dreaming of the day when they would be rich like George Hill and drive a motor car. Imagine not having to saddle up the old mare every Sunday and put her into the trap, but just to come out and sit into a car. George had let them look under the bonnet and explained the logistics of the engine. The boys were fascinated especially Seamus who had a keen interest in engines and any thing mechanical. Larry Devine had recently bought one of the new fangled tractors for the farm and Seamus spent every spare minute over with him Looking at the machine. He wished that they had more money and that his mother could buy a tractor and of course he would be the one to drive it. At ten Sean was too young but he was thirteen and three quarters, he could drive it with no bother. It was a happy group that traipsed off home, bringing Terence with them until they came to the shop. Goodbye Terry said Seamus we'll see you on Monday at school. Terence tore into the shop almost knocking his father down inside the door. Whoa where 's the fire Tom asked, The little boy looked up at his father his eyes shining, Daddy wait until I tell you he panted, This is its self was enough for Tom to stand quite still and look again at his son, the fact that Terence had even stopped to talk to him was riveting, but the words came tumbling out, I went for a drive with Mr. Hill, Kate's father he explained. Me and the Banaghans and it was great, we must have done a hundred miles an hour, Tom smiled to himself at the idea of the sedate George Hill tearing through the village at a hundred miles an hour, but he said nothing, the fact his son was telling him anything was in itself a miracle. I have something else to tell you Terence said excitedly, Tom sat down on the high stool he kept behind the counter in case he ever got a minute to himself, He looked at the little flushed face in front of him and suddenly a rush of love for his painfully shy boy filled his heart. What is this great news, Terence standing straight and proud. looked him in the eye and announced I am the best goal keeper in the school. Tom would have fallen off the high stool only he was holding on to the counter. You are, he said? Yes I am, Seamus Banaghan said so, I never let in one goal today and on

Monday I am to be in goals at school. Tom digested this piece of news with joy in his heart, were you playing football with the Banaghans he asked, yes you know my friends Lily and Kate, yes said his father whose heart was sore at the fact that the boy only ever seemed to be with these two girls, We were over there and Seamus made me goalie and Sean said I was the best ever, so I will be playing football with the boys on Monday, The girls are ok but us boys are better. It was the sweetest Sentence out of his son's mouth that Tom could have wished for. Hold on a minute he said I am going to shut the shop early and we will all have our dinner together for once. He pulled the ancient wooden blinds down on the door and took Terrence's hand as the two of them made their way up stairs together. Sally was just about to go down to let Tom up when the two arrived in the door hand in hand, It was hard to tell which face was beaming the most. Sally looked at them in astonishment as the girls ran to their father to put him in his chair. Amy and May sat him down and jumped into the chairs either side of him, Hold on a minute he said I need Terence to sit here beside me this evening as we have to discuss some of the finer points of Goalkeeping, Angela looked at her father as if he had two heads, Sally made to go down to the shop but was told to stay where she was by Tom, who announced that the place was shut and it was shut for the night. Terence, Angela snorted, he doesn't know the first thing about football, he never plays with the boys at school. Tom looked around at the four pairs of female eyes staring at Terence, who had suddenly lost his voice again. This boy was playing football today he announced, with the Banaghan Boys and they had him in goals, he never let in a ball, isn't that right son, he said giving him a pat on the shoulder, Sally looked on her heart in her mouth as she waited for Terence to answer, Suddenly as had Lizzie Banaghan's Floodgates opened in Mary Hill's house so did Terence's. I don't want to be called Terence any more I want to be called Terry it suits me better he said to the stunned audience of his sisters and mother , I will be the new goalie at school on Monday and Seamus and Sean think I have it in me to go on to play for the Parish. I might not have played football, Angela but I watched them every day, I know which way a ball is going to go and I just jump up and catch it. Tom sighed with content as Sally putting out the Dinner of Cabbage turnips and bacon said well now TERRY, will you take a bit of everything, yes please mam he said seriously, I have to grow you know.

Chapter Twelve

The tenth of June arrived with not a cloud in the sky.
The Parish Church was awash with bunting hanging
from the bell tower to the front Gates. Father Hoey was
at the Porch to welcome each and every one. Miss
Conlon was at the front of the Altar ushering the first
Communicant's into the Front seat and their parents
into the seats behind. The children had been fasting
from midnight and thought that they might die of the
hunger before they got the precious host. Mass was at
nine thirty and it would be at least another hour before
they got any breakfast. Tummy's were rattling between
nerves and hunger. Terence Sheehan was to lead the
children out from the seat when Miss Conlon gave the
nod to go to the Altar. She had put the names into a hat
and his had come out, Miss Conlon left to herself would
never have picked him, but he seemed different today,
his dickey bow and white suit gave him and air of
confidence which had been sadly lacking up until now,
Lily Banaghan was next and she looked absolutely
angelic in a beautiful white lace dress that looked like it
had come from fairyland. Kate also looked Angelic with
her blonde curls escaping from beneath her veil. They
were all very good and all six of the children received
their first Holy Communion with never a mistake
between them. Miss Conlon heaved a sigh of relief as
the choir sang Hail Holy Queen and Father Hoey and
Father Mc Govern preceded by the Altar boys headed
into the Sacristy. Once outside the three boys and three

girls lined up for George Hill to take their photograph. He was the only parent with a camera. It was the Brownie box camera that his friend and best man Charles Fuller gave him when he was leaving for Ireland. Goodbye old friend he had said, send me some pictures of your new life as he handed him the camera. George remembered guiltily that he never did send Charles any photos. Maybe he would send him one of Kate in her First Communion dress.

It was a quite gleeful party that arrived back at the Hill's house. Mary had been up early that morning and cooked bacon, black pudding and sausages, they were keeping warm in the oven of her new electric cooker. She was going to fry eggs as soon as she got everyone settled. Lizzie had brought over her brown bread the night before together with several little dishes of butter rolled and patterned, some homemade marmalade and strawberry jam, She also brought a big bowl of jelly with a jug of custard. My goodness Mary had exclaimed, this is lovely, thank you so much. No Mary, sighed Lizzie, thank you so much. The Banaghans were introduced to Mary's parents and brother Pat. Everyone chatted as if they had known each other for years. Annie Quinn was talking to Lizzie about the merit of bleaching the clothes by throwing them on to the nearest hedge and also the best way to churn the butter, Paddy Quinn and George were chatting about the cost of living, George earnestly telling Paddy how to manage his accounts with Paddy nodding his head and having not the slightest intention of taking George's advice. The children were out in the garden the Banaghan boys especially Seamus, were hoping to get George to show them the engine of the car again. Kate and Lily were walking up and down the path as if they were going to take off and fly away in their glorious white frothy dresses. Their friend Terry as he now wanted to be called would be coming over later when the Sheehans had finished their celebrations. His granny and grandad on his father's side were there as was his other grandad, his mother's father He was still friends with the girls but seemed to spend more time with Lily's brothers and the other boys than he did with them. Pat decided to go out and join the children. Well now aren't you two the beautiful young ladies he said to the girls as they paused in their parading. They giggled as he hunkered down beside them. Here is a half a crown for each of you he said as he took the money out of his pocket, spend it wisely and don't spend it all on ice cream he laughed. They both said thank you and Lily who had never had so much money in her life ran in to give it to her mother. Lizzie was astounded at the generosity of Mary's brother whom they had only just met. We can't possibly take this from your brother she said to Mary, Don't be daft said Mary sure he has lots of it and he would be insulted if you didn't take it. Lizzie said no more, but resolved to thank Pat when he came back in. Pat in the meantime had Kate up on his shoulders giving her a piggy back ride. She held on to his auburn curls for dear life, you are pulling my hair from its roots he laughed, sorry uncle Pat said Kate putting her arms around his neck instead. You have hair just like my cousin Patrick she said as he tickled her, Pat put her down on the ground, you have a cousin Patrick he said puzzled as he knew George was an only child, yes he lives with my Auntie Molly in England, she's not really my Aunt she's my Godmother. He has hair just like yours, in fact he looks like you she said, running off into the house to find Lily. Pat's world tilted as he sat down with a bang amongst the rose bushes in Mary's garden. Molly had a child, Kate knew them, how old was this child that looked like him. He had to get Kate on her own again even though it wasn't fair to be picking information out of her.

After a wonderful breakfast Paddy Quinn lay back in his chair and announced that he was as full as a tick and would in fact never need to eat again. Kate and Lily laughed at him, what's a tick Grandad asked Kate getting up on his lap. Well now Lily, will we tell her what a tick is ? Lily knew all too well what a tick was having had her mother pinch them out of her arms and legs many times after a long day in the meadow. Paddy looked at her earnest little face and pulling her up onto his lap beside Kate he said well as full as I am, I still have room on my lap for the two prettiest girls in the Parish. Lizzie Banaghan was delighted for Lily as there was really no male influence in her little girls' life apart from her older brothers, who were not bad boys but sometimes she worried about the loss of a male point of view for her boys as well. She was feeling very relaxed, the most of the days work on her farm was being done by Larry Devine, and she would repay him in kind when he needed her. She so seldom had the luxury of sitting and just watching her children in such a happy atmosphere that the hollows in her cheeks seem to have filled out and her newly washed hair hung in waves around her face and made her feel human again. She was very grateful to Mary and George for having them and she said so now to Mary who was pressing her to have another cup of tea. The Sheehans were coming over when Toms Parents left for home. Pat knew he would never get Kate on her own again today, he would have to bide his time and think about what he was going to do. He was in a fog of memories as the talk and madness of laughing children passed over his head as he sat in a daze. Mary looked at him a few times wondering what was up with him, she was about to go over to him when Angela Sheehan came bursting in the door. Mrs Hill we can't come over, Mammy is having the baby and everyone is gone mad over there. Granny is upstairs with mammy and she said I was to come over and tell you that we can't come, Mary and Lizzie sprung into action, Come in, Angela you sit down here, we will bring over Terry and the twins, There is plenty of food and we are having a great time. Angela sank into the first chair inside the door with relief Kate looked at her with envy imagine having twin sisters and Terry and now she was getting another baby sister or brother. How lucky she was. Angela at that time was having no such thoughts, she had seen her mother writhing on the bed in agony while her granny Rose held on to her arms. Get out of here Sally had screamed at Angela, her hair plastered to her forehead, go over to Hills and tell them we are not coming over. Angela ran. Her father, Terry and the twins were sitting at the long table that Tom had set up in the closed shop where the remains of the half eaten breakfast congealed on the plates. Sally's father Tim Carey and Tom's Father Terence sat smoking their pipes as they discussed the price of cattle oblivious to the drama being played out in the bedroom. Tom felt sick in his stomach, he knew Sally wanted this baby and so did he, half heartedly, he had to admit. They were struggling enough with the four they had, but at this moment he just wanted it to be over and for Sally and the baby to be all right. Mary Hill knocked at the shop door, as she stooped down to shout in the letterbox, its only Mary and I have Lizzie Banaghan with me, let us in Tom, Tom gratefully open the door and the women and took over the shambles immediately. Off with the lot of you over to our house Mary said as she got inside surveying the half eaten breakfast. There is plenty of food and my mam has the kettle boiling take the twins and Terry with you Tom, as well as the pipe smoking grandfathers in the corner. We will send over word as soon as there is any news. Lizzie was already tidying up the Table while Mary took the stairs two at a time, Sally was having pains almost every minute and her competent mother-in-law was in full control, Won't be long now she said to Mary who held back at the door, her own confinement coming back into her head with a vengeance even after seven years. What can I do she whispered, you can get the cradle ready, the baby blankets are in the dressing table drawer. There are baby gowns and nappies in there as well, Mary did as she was bid, praying for Sally's ordeal to be over soon. Rose Sheehan was in her element, having delivered babies all over her home Parish but this was the first time she had delivered a grandchild. The baby was three weeks early but hopefully it would be smaller and be easier on Sally who by now was exhausted but calm as she knew the baby was almost here, she could feel the head emerging and with a last push her second son and last child was born roaring his lungs out. Will you look at the size of him said Rose handing him over to Sally, it's a good job he didn't go another three weeks in there or you would have to get a rope to pull him out. Sally collapsed back on to the pillows laughing, she was very fond of her mother-in-law and her dry wit. Mary gaped at her she didn't remember laughing for at least a week after Kate was born, she was so sore. You are wonderful she said to Sally as she hugged her and the baby in one big armful. No Indeed, Sally said, Rose is the wonderful one here. Thank you so much Mam-in-law. Rose beamed, taking the baby and carefully putting him into his gown and placing him into the cradle. We will get you tidied up and then let the hoards descend on you for a few minutes. You need to rest a grath and get your strength back.

Mary went back to tell Tom and the rest of the family about the safe arrival of the new baby. Lizzie who had the shop tidied up and shining like a new pin stayed on with Rose to get the bedroom in shape for the visitors. Hills house was a bit crazy as Mary went in the door. Paddy Quinn together with Tom, Terrence Sheehan Snr, and Tim Carey were playing cards at the table, they were trying to teach George the rudiments of twenty five, he got more bewildered as the game went on, with the banging of the table when a trick was got and the placing of matches in each player's place to mark how many tricks they had, he didn't think he would ever get the hang of the game and although Annie didn't approve of cards she said nothing as she knew it would be a distraction from all the goings on over at Sheehans. Pat had all of the children sitting on the floor and they were in teams, girls versus boys guessing the various questions that he threw at them. Annie was adding up the scores, the teams were even and the last question Pat threw at them was, would the baby be a boy or a girl. There was pandemonium as they squabbled and argued the Banaghan boys said of course it will be a boy while Terry wasn't so sure, he already had three sisters so the odds weren't looking too good. The twins decided it would be a girl, while Angela thoughtfully said she would like it to be a boy for Terry's sake, Lily and Kate were making up their minds when Mary came in the door, The game was abandoned as they all looked expectantly at her. It's a beautiful baby boy and mother and baby are well. Go ahead over Tom and the rest of you can go later. Terry was over the moon, at last he had a brother of his very own, he could teach him to play football and bring him places without trailing after the girls. The twins soon got over their disappointment at not having another sister and everyone started talking at once. Pat announced there would be an additional question and it would be that who ever guessed the name of the new baby would get a ten shilling note. Annie smiled at her son, he was very good with children she thought sadly it's such a pity he doesn't have any of his own. The naming ceremony raged on and on , James Michael, Peter, John all were thrown into the hat, everyone wanted to win the money, George who by now had abandoned the card game much to the relief of the other players, said I will match that with another ten shillings, Terry who had been very quiet during the squabble over names suddenly spoke up, I think he should be called Corpus Christi Sheehan, because that is today's feast day. Even Annie laughed at the seriousness of Terry's chosen names. We will have to wait and see she said, Your daddy is going over now and will be back for you in a bit so I am going to make up some food for your mammy who must be starving, be very good when you go into her and no fighting over names. She needs a bit of peace and quiet.

Tom and Sally looked at their sleeping son, Thank you love said Tom who was in his way romantic enough when they were on their own, he is a handsome fellow and Terence, I mean Terry is thrilled to have a brother and so are the girls they will all be here on top of you in a minute he said as I promised them I would go for them as quick as I could, but at the moment they are guessing his name. What have you in mind love he said as he laughingly told her of Terry's suggestion that the baby be called Corpus Christi Sheehan. Well Tom I was thinking of Thomas after yourself, we can add Christopher but he will be called Christy to avoid confusion with two Toms, that way Terry will have had a hand in his name. Tom heartily agreed and so it was that Terry got the two ten shilling notes with which he bought football togs and boots from Mrs Canny as soon as the shop was open. He bought the boots in a size two even though he only took a size one as he figured out by the time he got to play for the Parish he would be a size two, Mrs Canny tried to make him get the right size, but he was adamant, so she agreed on condition that if he didn't wear them and kept them in the box, and if the Parish suddenly decided they needed a size one boot goalie, that she would change them. Terry gravely thanked her as he shook her hand, He wasn't sure if should spit on his hand or not as he had seen Larry Devine do when he was making a bargain at the cattle fair. He wisely decided against the spit as he figured a lady mightn't like it.

Chapter Thirteen

The first Communion day went down in history in the minds of everyone at it, for many different reasons, It was the first Communion day but it was also the birthday of Christy Sheehan, it was, in Georges mind the day in which he resolved never to play any more cards, he would disappear immediately if he ever say anyone with a pack of cards in their hand again. It was the day that Lizzie Banaghan felt like herself for the first time since her husband died, It was the day that Mary Hill decided that maybe they should have another baby, she had seen how enthusiastic Kate had been about Christy Sheehan and how envious she was of her friend's who had brothers and sisters. She would have to work on George as he was quite happy himself to be an only child and had always been so. It would be the day in Pat Quinn's mind that he found out he was a father and that Molly was somewhere near where Mary and George had lived in England. He had gone over in his head a thousand times, Kate's words, " you have hair like my cousin Patrick in fact he looks like you. He lives with my Auntie Molly." He didn't get to have any more conversation with his niece with all the craziness of the Communion day. He wouldn't see her for a while but he was steadily making plans in his head. What would his parents think, they would be so disappointed in him, Doctor Mc Gee would kill him, How would he get Molly to marry him, how would he get her to come back to Ireland. He couldn't possibly live in England, it would break his parent's hearts and both His parents and all the neighbours would consider his son a bastard. How in the name of God was he going to put this right. Could he ever put it right. He couldn't sleep at night, he couldn't eat, even his parents noticed how silent and withdrawn he had become.

Mary and George were sitting in the front room, they had just had their Sunday dinner and Kate had gone over to Lily's house, she was either over at Banaghans or in Sheehans playing with Christy as Terry was out all the time practising his football skills. Don't you think it would be nice if Kate had a brother or sister she suddenly threw into the conversation. George looked at her in astonishment, what would she want anybody else for, he said, she has lots of friends and she is a very happy little girl. I grew up on my own and I was quite happy. I know you did said Mary putting her arms around him, but just think how nice it would be to have a baby in the house and how great it would be for Kate. We are not stuck for money. We have lots of room, My parents would love another grandchild, please say yes she pleaded. George looked at her reflectively, is this some Catholic thing where you must have more than one child he asked, he knew all about the Church's wish to procreate, and even though he knew his mother-in-law had forgiven him for being a protestant and for marrying Mary he was not immune to the hints she had given about more babies. Mary was horrified at the idea that there was anything devious in the fact that she wanted another child. No, she cried how could you think I would even go along with such nonsense, forget I ever said anything. I am quite happy with my Kate. George was in a reflective mood all day, he realised that even though Kate was a very happy little girl, that she spent as much, if not more time in the houses of their neighbour's children, where she seemed to enjoy the rough and tumble of their siblings. He would quite like a son he realised but then he wouldn't mind another daughter either.

Terry tried on his football boots every morning and then put them back into the box. He played football like every other boy in school in his bare feet. If he did get to play for the Parish, he hoped it would be soon.He wished Christy would grow a bit faster as it seemed that having a brother didn't seem to make much difference at the moment. His brother was a happy baby and he did make them all laugh at his goo goo sounds as he tried to talk baby talk. His mammy spent most of her time changing his nappies or washing his nappies or bringing him for walks to get fresh air into him, The girls were over their initial delight at having a baby in the house and moaned when they were asked to rock him or give him a bottle. Tom did his best to help but as the bulk of the shop work fell on him now he wasn't able to do much. They were both exhausted and as Sally told Mary when she called in to see how Christy was doing she would give anything for a full nights sleep. Oh you poor thing Mary exclaimed, why don't you go and have a lie down now and I will bring Christy for a walk.Sally gratefully took her up on the offer, Oh that would be wonderful she said, just give me an hour and I'll be a new woman. Sally carefully manoeuvred the ancient pram down the stairs through the shop where she told Tom she was going to give Sally a few hours sleep, while the children were at school. Tom was happy for Sally as he wearily thought how nice it would be to put his head down too. The shop door opened with a ping and he knew that the likelihood of a rest was as remote as a lighthouse. Mary sauntered off into the sunshine pretending that Christy was her baby and thinking how broody she was feeling

George was at a meeting with the firm's Managing Director, Cecil Atkins, the firm was doing very well and expansion was at the top of the agenda, The fact that the M.D. had taken time out from his busy schedule in England was not lost on George. The village of Ballybrae was in a great position for Road and rail travel to Dublin, Ireland's Capital City Cecil said, the firm have decided that having reviewed the area census that the population warranted a much needed boost to the work starved area. The business would be a benefit to both men and women who wanted to stay in their own environment. Each Year hundreds of young Irish people were taking the boat to Britain or America through lack of employment at home. They were putting George in Charge, It would mean that he was responsible for the plant in Ballybrae, It would mean a lot more money for him as well as responsibility, but George knew he was well fit for the job, in fact he couldn't wait to get stuck in. He thanked The M.D. and assured him of his very best performance. Cecil Atkins liked George, he knew from his track record that the firm of P.C. Daws Ltd was in good hands. He shook hands with George wondering how anyone could possibly be happy to work in this backwater. He pulled the collar of his Harris tweed coat up around his ears as he stepped into his hired car, glad to be on his way to Dublin to catch a plane back to London and civilisation.

George was elated, he knew by now how immigration was affecting families in the Country, he also knew that most Irish Farmers left the farm to the oldest son or to the one that stayed at home. The recipient of the farm however was expected to keep his parents in the house even if he decided to marry and also that his new bride would have to get on with her parents -in-law there was no such thing as divorce or the new bride becoming "boss" in her home. it would be the territory of the mother -in-law until the day she died or maybe if a daughter took her off to live with her. The Father would have to be consulted on every moo, grunt and cackle of the livestock. It was a no win situation for most of the young men and women who stayed at home. Having a job locally would be, in Georges mind a solution to a lot of people's problems. When the new extension was up and running it would give employment for many around Ballybrae.It would keep the population at home and boost the economy, He was so happy to be part of this project that he couldn't wait to get home to tell Mary of this new development.

Mary was very happy for her husband whose enthusiasm was catching, Maybe People like Lizzie Banaghan and the Sheehans would be able to keep their children at home instead of crying goodbye to them as they sailed away she said. Yes George agreed and we will have apprenticeships for young lads so that they can learn the trade if they don't have the necessary cash or academic qualities to continue their education. I have so many plans Mary, I am so glad that we live in this beautiful place and can bring hope to people who need it. One thing sure our children will grow up in a happy and safe environment with opportunities to do whatever they want. Mary looked at him in astonishment, our children she quoted, yes my love, we will have as many as you want he laughed. Well now hold on there Mary replied I only said I would like another baby not a whole parcel of them, but she was so happy that she ran over to her husband and with a blissful sigh and thanked God for such a wonderful man.

Seamus Banaghan was looking into the engine of Larry Devine's tractor as Larry reved it up and shouted at him to take his head up out of the way. Larry laughed at the boy's enthusiasm and knew that at fourteen he was too young to get a driving licence, but he thought it would be no harm since the boy was so enthusiastic to let him drive for a bit around the bull's field. It was flat and even and there was no bull in it. It was called the bull's field after some long distant time when Larry's father kept a bull. Come on son he said to Seamus, if you are very careful, I will let you drive around the field once. Seamus needed no second bidding as he hastily abandoned the bonnet of the tractor and jumped up into the bucket seat. Larry banged the bonnet down and jumping up behind Seamus he showed him how to start the tractor and which lever to push with his foot. He showed him the brake and he stood carefully behind Seamus as they stuttered off to a shaky start. The young lad was a fast learner and by the time they had done a lap of the Field he was in full possession. Please Larry can we do it once more he begged, go on then said Larry just once and then you had better be off home or your mother will be wondering where you are. They were just pulling up to the gate at the road when the said mother suddenly came running in and stood with her mouth agape as Seamus pulled up beside her. She was furious, what is wrong with you Larry Devine she roared, have you taken leave of your senses, he is fourteen for God's sake, she pulled the frightened looking boy down off the tractor, he had never seen his mammy so mad, neither had Larry Devine, Lizzie looked magnificent, her hair falling out of it's habitual bun and around her face like a halo, she went for Larry like a virago giving him several thumps on the chest, he caught her arms as she was making for his head, It's all right Lizzie he said looking at her earnestly, I would never let Seamus do anything dangerous. I was with him all the time and we never left the field. You do know that I am fierce fond of Seamus and I swear he Won't do it again if you don't want him to. Lizzie was beginning to calm down when she realised her son was really in no danger and she believed Larry when he said he was fond of her son, she realised that she was still being held by the arms of the man she was after walloping around the place. She hastily tried to bundle her hair out of her eyes. Suddenly Larry shocked both himself and lizzie by saying softly, leave your hair down, it looks lovely. They were both frozen in disbelief at Larry's words. He had never once looked at a woman never mind comment on her hair. He was a good man and had looked after both his parents for as long as they lived. He had never had the pleasure of going out to enjoy himself when they were alive and didn't know how to after they died. He enjoyed helping out at Banaghans after Denis had passed away from T.B., he loved it when the children came over and had appreciated Lizzie's help when he had the station Mass. He now pulled back from her in shock and Lizzie suddenly felt bereft when he took his hands from her arms, she shook herself in horror at this disloyal feeling to Denis. Get on home with you Seamus she said looking around for her son, who had long gone, running as fast as his legs would carry him when he saw his mother attacking their neighbour. She looked back at Larry who was still standing where she had left him, I'm sorry for clattering you she said but I don't think Seamus should be driving that tractor. Larry nodded his head and walked away from her without uttering another word.

Lizzie was sitting in Mary Hill's kitchen, they were both in the choir and Lizzie had called for Mary on her way up to the practice. Lily had come with her and was going to stay and play with Kate. Sally Sheehan was also going with them having coaxed Angela into minding Christy who was growing fast and now had several teeth. Mary came downstairs as George was asking Lizzie would she like a cup of coffee. Lizzie didn't like to say she never tasted coffee before, but she didn't get a chance as Mary rushed her out the door, come on she said or we will be late, Lizzie looked at her in surprise as they had plenty of time but she obediently got up and said nothing. They went into Sheehans and Tom called out to Sally who came flying down pulling her coat on as she gave directions, right left and centre, Tom make sure you check on Angela, she is listening to Radio Luxemburg and will forget all about Christy, the twins are due home in half an hour and Terry will be back soon after that. Their dinners are in the oven and I Won't be any more than an hour. Tom looked at her affectionately, he was glad to see her get away for a bit but he forgot all the instructions as soon as she was gone out the door. Are you two early or is my clock slow she asked as they made their way up the street. Lizzie looked at Mary who was bursting to tell them her news, we are early she said it's just that I have something to tell you, The two women looked at her expectantly, I am having another baby, she stated her face radiant with happiness. Her friends were delighted for her and both hugged her as they reached the Church. Kate will be thrilled said Sally, I know said Mary, but please don't say anything as I havn't told her the news. Mary and George were delighted and surprised when Mary got pregnant so quickly, they hadn't even told the grandparents yet, but Mary just had to tell her friends or she would have busted keeping it to herself. She had also Written to Molly to tell her the news and was waiting for a reply. She had thought long and hard about what to say in the letter as she knew it would be hard on Molly, but there was no way to plaster it over so she had come straight out with it. Baby Hill no 2 is on the way please think seriously about coming over for the birth. I really want you here. He/she is due late next February. The choir practice over, the friends excitedly chattered on about Mary's news. Are you hoping for a boy or girl asked Sally. We both honestly don't mind, George is very happy with either and so am I. Kate Won't care so long as it's a baby she laughed. Now that's enough about me, we so seldom get to chat without busy little ears listening in, have any of you got any news, Sally laughed well unless you consider Christy's new tooth news That's about it with me. They both looked at Lizzie who 's mouth took on a voice of its own as it announced Larry Devine said my hair was lovely. The sky didn't fall but the two women with her nearly did as they bumped into each other in astonishment. What shrieked Sally, Larry Devine who never looked at a woman in his life, never mind her hair, when was this, come on you have to tell us. Lizzie who by now was bright red with embarrassment was as shocked as the others when the words came out of her mouth, It was the other evening when I went over for Seamus who is always hanging out of Larry's tractor, I caught the two of them in the Bull's field with Seamus driving the bloody thing and I tore into Larry and battered the head of him, My hair fell down with the shaking I was giving him and I tried to stuff it back up and then he had me by the arms and said it was lovely and to leave it down. I have it nearly glued on to my head since in case it comes down and he thinks I let it down for him, the other too laughed at her until they looked at her woebegone face. Isn't it great that you have a fine man like that hankering after you said Mary seriously? I didn't say he was hankering after me shouted Lizzie looking so fierce that Mary pulled back. Ok she said but its about time you had a life and it's about time that poor Larry knew what it was like to run his hands through your hair. Lizzie went off home in a sulk although it wasn't really Mary she was mad at, it was herself for going faint at the thought of Larry Devine running his hands through her hair. What would people think, what would the children think and rather belatedly she thought what would Denis think.

Chapter Fourteen

The Parish sports were held in August each year and it was one of the highlights of local life. There were races for children of all ages with medals to be won. There were three legged races and regular races, There was tossing the sheaf, tug o' war where the strong and not so strong men of the area pitted their strength against each other, there was a dog show, a Punch and Judy show, a football match against the next Parish, a display of Irish step dancing, a cookery competition where you could get a rosette for brown bread, apple tart or for the best fairy cakes or sponge cake. There was a Marquee that sold tea and sandwiches and an old caravan always pulled up the night before with a fortune teller named Madame Zelda. Kate and Lily were performing a two-hand reel and a double jig, they had the floor almost worn out in Hills hallway practising, The twins and Angela were dancing a hornpipe and a three hand reel. The hornpipe being much superior to the reel and double jig as Amy informed Kate. The boys were all competing in the races and the most wonderful news of all Terry was the new goalie in the under ten football match. All that was needed to make the day perfect was sunshine. Father Hoey even prayed at 9.30 Mass that the day would be good and he wished the Parish team the best of luck in the Match and seeing as how some of the boys including Terry were serving Mass that morning, they were bursting with pride. Annie and Paddy Quinn had been prevailed upon by Mary to come up on a holiday for a couple of weeks, you can see Kate dancing and meet all of our friends at the sports and I have some news to tell you Mary wrote. Pat who was listening to his mother read out the letter suddenly perked up, of course you will go mam a little holiday will do yourself and dad a world of good and Kate will be thrilled to see her granny and granddad. Annie looked reflectively at Pat who had become so thin and withdrawn lately, that she was at her wits end. I think myself that it is you that needs the holiday she remarked, isn't that right Paddy, she said to her husband who was sitting at the end of the table finishing his breakfast. Pat was having none of it, sure the hay is saved, the turf is in, there is nothing to worry about and sure Won't I have a great time here with you two gone and me with a whole house to myself. Paddy looked keenly at his son and spoke up, I think we should go Annie he said quietly thinking to himself that maybe Pat did need a bit of space, he hadn't been himself lately and Paddy would really like to see Mary, Kate and George. That's settled so said Pat, write to Mary and I will post the letter for you as I am going past the post office on the way for meal for the hens. Pat went off to change his clothes and when he came back the letter was on the table. He put it in his pocket and headed off before Annie could change her mind. He went into the post office to get the stamp. The postmistress Mrs Corr was stamping a parcel. Good day Pat she said is it a stamp you are wanting looking at the letter in his hand. It is indeed Mrs Corr said Pat, but I also want to book a ticket on the boat for Holyhead. Mrs Corr looked at him in surprise but she was the soul of discretion and no one had heard a whisper of anybody else's business from her. Pat knew this or he would have gone in to Carrickmore where people didn't care where you went. I need a return he said hoping that nobody else would come in until his business was done. I will travel on the fourteenth of August and come back on the 19th he said.his parents were away until the twenty first, that should give him plenty of time to locate Molly and her boy. He couldn't bring himself to think of him as his until he actually saw him and until Molly told him the truth.

Pat posted the letter to Mary, got the meal for the hens in the Creamery and headed not for home but over to Jim Collins who was raking rushes in the front field as he walked up. Jim he said can I talk to you a minute, I need a big favour. Jim looked at his neighbour and knew something was troubling him, come away into the house he said Kitty and the boys are gone to her mother for the day, I am sick of raking these rushes anyway and I could do with a cup of tea. The kettle was bubbling away on the range as they went into the kitchen, sit down there now Jim said, Kitty left some nice brown scones for my tea. Pat waited until the tea was made and the butter and scones produced, he suddenly felt hungry and he knew it was because he might be nearer to finding a solution to his problem. I need you to look after our place for a few days next week, Mam and dad are going up to Mary for a bit of a break and I am going over to England for a few days. Jim chewed steadily not speaking, he knew there was more to come, It's just the cattle and the hens he said, the cat can catch mice and if you throw a bit to the two dogs that would be great. I will do the same for you if you ever need me to. Jim rubbed his beard and waited he knew there was more. Do you remember that night long ago when my sister and her friend Molly Mc Gee went to the Parish dance after their leaving cert and you asked me if you could walk Mary home? Jim spoke up at last, indeed and I do, she was the first girl I ever kissed and you nearly frightened the life out me when you came rushing up with Molly and bundled me off home. Well I did something then that has haunted me ever since. He stopped for breath I was going to break it off with Molly that night, we had being seeing each other all Summer and I knew that she was too young and innocent for me , when yourself and Mary went up to the house we went in to Meehan's hayshed and I lost the run of myself, she was so trusting but I in my wisdom afterwards, told her to go off and learn about life, meet someone her own age and forget about me. Then herself and Mary went off on holiday to England and got stuck in the war. Mary married George and of course you met himself and Kate when they came over for one of your kittens. Jim nodded, he knew there was more by the way Pat was shifting himself about on the chair. Well to get to the crunch of the story, I did ask Mary about Molly and why she never came home but she was quite evasive and gave me an answer that was no answer. Kate however blew my world apart one day when she told me about her cousin, in England who had hair like mine and in fact looked just like me. Now you know why Molly never came back, she had my baby, she couldn't come back. Jim looked at him, are you sure that you have all the facts, did you ask Mary. No Pat was adamant that he wasn't going to do that as he didn't trust his sister not to warn Molly and that she would disappear and be lost to him a second time. What are you going to do in England Jim asked mildly, its quite a big place. Pat allowed himself a glimmer of a smile, I know that, but I also know where Mary lived and according to Kate, Molly and Patrick lived close by. She called him Patrick said Jim in surprise, not a good plan if you are trying to hide. I know Pat said, I was a bit surprised myself at that also. Well all will be well here, I will make sure of that my friend said Jim sticking out his hand to Pat, Pat took it gratefully. The thing is I don't really know what to do if I find them. Even if she still loves me and agrees to marry me I can't suddenly tell my mam here is your grandson. You know what she's like and I can't walk up the Church on Sunday with my wife and son in tow. What am I going to do. Jim lit a cigarette and pulled long and hard on it. Well he said times are changing, you certainly couldn't have got away with it ten years ago in the forties but sure we are well into the fifties now and things are getting more relaxed, but sure it will only be a one week wonder. Go on over and see how it goes, Molly may cut the ground from under you and want nothing to do with marrying or the like. Things may be changing Pat said, but My mother nearly went mad when she found out that Mary had married a protestant, she nearly took the door off the Parochial House in her haste to get them married in the Catholic Church. Pat had told Jim things that he had never divulged to a single soul and he knew instinctively that Jim wouldn't say a word. Well the best of luck my friend Jim said still shaking Pat's hand, I for one would be delighted to welcome both you and Molly here and also the wee lad he added hastily. Pat took the hand and hoped that he would be able to repay Jim for his kindness someday. He now had to go home and pack a few things and take a journey that he hoped would change his life.

The day of the sports arrived the sun shone, Larry Devine's field was mowed within an inch of it's life. The markings for the football pitch and the sports area were all chalked out in white. The marquee was adorned with yellow and maroon bunting, the Parish colours. Chairs were brought down from the hall for any elderly people who might like to sit down for the cup of tea. The dancing took place on the back of the old creamery Lorry where Frank Healy played the fiddle accompanied by Jane O' Reilly on the accordion. The Tannoy system was in place and all was in order. Kate Hill and Lily Banaghan were wearing green pleated skirts and White blouses, they had two large green ribbons on either side of their hair, so large that it looked like they might take flight. The Sheehan twins and Angela had bainin dancing dresses courtesy of Mrs Canny, the dresses were stiff with embroidery and their hair was stiff with ringlets from the previous nights twisting of rags around them that took Sally two hours. They also had little aprons in front with the medals they had won at various other Feiseanna and sports. They were magnificent and Tom who had come up from the shop which he was closing for the day looked at them with pride, he was waiting for his son to come down from the attic in his football gear and as Terry came bursting in wearing the correct sized boots courtesy also of Mrs Canny Tom's heart overflowed with pride in his family he put his arm around Sally as she picked up Christy from the cot. Thank you my love he whispered. Sally knew enough not to answer or the two of them would be making a show of themselves, come on she said let's go, and the Sheehan family in all their glory headed out the door for Devine's Field.

George Hill had been asked to be a judge at the tug o' war and also the dog show, he declined the tug o' war saying he knew nothing about the rules but agreed to judge the dogs. Mary. Lizzie and Sally were helping out in the marquee but were getting time off to watch the dancing and of course Sally was going to watch the football. When the Parish priest heard that Mary's Mother was coming he requested that she judge the baking as she would be an outsider and be considered a fair choice. Annie was thrilled and had her best Sunday go to Mass hat, two piece suit and shoes with the Cuban heels on.Mary had told her parents the night before about the new grandchild and the Quinns were also bursting with happiness, Herself and George had told Kate about the new brother or sister before her granny and granddad arrived, she was so happy and couldn't wait to get out to tell Lily the news. Lizzie Banaghan had on a new blue dress the exact colour of her eyes, she had been up in Mary's house the previous week and

146

Mary presented her with the dress, it Won't fit me as I am getting big around the waist and it would look better on you anyway. Mary stated, please don't say no and for God's sake let your hair down and I'mean literally as well as properly she said, come up to me the night before the sports and I will put curlers in your hair, you must have a headache with that bun screwed up on your head all the time. Lizzie gulped at Mary's generosity, she was dubious about letting down the hair but agreed to take the dress. Mary was having none of it, you can't have the dress unless you let me do your hair. Lily gave up she knew how persistent Mary could be. Ok she said resignedly, I will wear my hair down but I'm not having curlers in. Mary had to be content with that. It was the day of the sports and her children stared at her as she came into the kitchen in the blue dress, her newly washed shiny hair framing her face. Are you all ready for the Sports Lizzie asked, oh mam you look beautiful Lily said as she ran to give her mother a hug. Seamus looked at her from the lofty height of his fourteen years, you do like nice Mam he said you look younger or something, Sean thought she always looked lovely anyway, she was his Mammy and he loved her.

 Larry Devine was on the gate taking the entry money. He gave the Bull's field every year for free to the sports Committee and half the money taken on the gate went into Parish funds. He was delighted that the day was good as it meant that the field was dry and would make for a much better crowd. He opened the gate to let in the creamery lorry as it was only one of three vehicles allowed on the field Madame Zelda's caravan and the ice cream van being the other two. He could see her fixing her sign outside her caravan. It said HAVE YOUR FORTUNE TOLD. LEARN YOUR DESTINY.ALL FOR ONE SHILLING. Some people believed this nonsense, he knew and there would be queue of people mostly young girls later on but you wouldn't catch him going in there, he knew his destiny, it was right here in this field and the rest of his farm. He was standing looking at the fortune teller's caravan when Lizzie Banaghan and her children arrived at the gate. He was stunned at the beauty of Lizzie in the blue dress and her hair falling in waves around her shoulders, He hastily stopped staring as Seamus started talking to him about the tractor. Lizzie blushed at how she had behaved the evening that she had pulled her son from the machine. She tried not to look at Larry's strong arms as she put the money into the box. Larry tried and failed not to look at her again, but he couldn't stop himself, Lily who was anxious to get in to meet Kate looked at both of them, hurry up Mammy, I want to go in. The moment was broken but not before both Larry and Lizzie knew something had changed. Thank you, she said as Larry handed her the change, his hand almost scorching both of them as he touched her fingers. The children ran in and Lizzie ran after them like as if the devil was after her, she almost knocked down George Hill as he made his way over to the dog judging, Steady on old girl, George said putting out a hand to steady her, he thought she looked very well today and being English he told her so. Most Irish men wouldn't have noticed Lizzie thought and if they did wouldn't have said anything anyway. Thank you

Lizzie stammered not being in the habit of receiving compliments. It was the first of many that came her way that day. Sally and Mary were united in their attempts to bolster her confidence and to put it into her head that she was young and alive and didn't have to mourn for the rest of her life. They were determined that they would all visit Madame Zelda before the day was out as Mary knew that Lizzie would never go on her own. The dancing was about to start and the women made their way over to the Lorry where Frank Healy could be heard tuning his fiddle. The air of excitement was palpable. The younger girls were on first and Kate came running over to her mother. Mammy I can't believe I didn't want to live here, I don't miss Ballet and I just love the Irish dancing we are on in a minute and there are three other pairs of dancers. We have to bow to the crowd at the end of the dance and then go over to the judges. There was a big box in place for the dancers to step up onto the lorry and as the girls were on first, Mary helped them up on to it. Good luck she said as they bounded along the length of the platform. Frank and Jane played "St. Patrick's Day in the morning" as they did the double jig and then it was straight on to "Mrs Mc Clouds Reel". They were perfect until the end when having being told to bow to the crowd and there were three sides to the lorry they weren't sure which side to go and Lily went one way and Kate the other, the audience didn't seem to mind at all and the dancers were clapped and cheered as they left the stage. The judges were kind and told them to wait until the end, and the winners would be announced. They didn't win any medals but received highly commended certificates. They were delighted with themselves and even the fact that the Sheehan girls won the cup for their performance couldn't dim the enjoyment of the day. They went off to watch the Punch and Judy show licking their ice creams before they melted in the hot sun.

Annie Quinn wiped her brow, she was roasting in the hot marquee where the Cookery competition was taking place, her new shoes were pinching and the hat was giving her a headache. She was longing to get out into the sunshine and talk to Mary about the new grandchild. She had accepted that George was not a catholic but was a bit worried in case Mary didn't realise the importance of having the new baby baptised in the Catholic Church. Paddy told her to go easy on Mary and not be annoying her head about things as the baby wasn't due until February, but Annie liked to dot the i ' s and mark the t 's in time. She was also worried about Pat and how he never seemed to be happy these days, in fact he was like a bear with a sore head. Her headache was turning in to a fully fledged head banger, when Nell Canny from the shop came into the Marquee. Musha God help you, you're boiling altogether in the heat here, Take off your hat and let the breeze onto your head, nobody will pass a bit of heed and I see you have the high heels on too, sure you'll break your neck walking around the grass in them things. I think you are a size six she said pulling a pair of white sandals out of her bag like a magician pulling a rabbit out of a hat, I have been coming here a long time and always feel sorry for the lady judges who have to dress up like a dog's dinner especially when it's a hot day and the marquee is like a furnace. Annie gasped with relief as she eased off her shoes although she was still smarting a bit about being likened to a dog's dinner. She thanked Nell gratefully as she slipped off her shoes and put the sandals on, I had better leave on the hat she said in case his Reverence comes in. Nell laughed, you Won't catch him coming in here, he will be down at the tug o 'war , he is refereeing that as your son-in-law wasn't too sure of the rules. Annie took off the hat and her headache seemed to disappear along with it, I will pay you for the sandals when the judging is over. There is no hurry agrath sure I always have a supply of stock in my bag Nell Canny announced as if it was the most natural thing in the world. Mary had told her before about Mrs Canny being the treasure of the village and Annie could now see why. She continued on Tasting and placing 1st 2nd and 3rd rosettes where she saw fit and was happily putting on the last one when Kate came bouncing in with Lily in tow, look Granny we got certificates for our dancing and the judges highly commended us. Well now, that is wonderful, Annie beamed at her Grand daughter, she was such a lovely little girl, she wished Pat would get married and have children that she would be able to have total access to, but he never seemed to look at any of the local girls at all and the more she thought about his morose behaviour of late she couldn't see much prospect of any daughter-in-law coming along. Are you finishing judging these cakes Granny, do you want to come and watch the football. Annie once again thanked Nell Canny as she left the marquee with the girls chattering beside her. Mary looked up in astonishment from where she was pouring out teas as her hatless mother sauntered by with her jacket slung over her shoulders in a pair of sandals with her toes out. Times were surely changing.

The dog show was over as was the tug o 'war, Barking had now ceased as dogs were fed by their proud owners. The local Tug o ' war team had unfortunately been beaten by Drumsna who were well known for their prowess on the tug o 'war front. It didn't stop the enjoyment of the day as both teams headed for the Marquee for tea and ham sandwiches. Most people were now heading over to the top of the field where the sports was just finishing up with the U16 Races. The U10 Football match was in the second half. Tom Sheehan was an umpire and he wiped the sweat from his brow as the U tens from Carrickmore seemed to be everywhere. The Kilmacden boys were doing their best but needed a surge of luck now as much as good footballing skill. Seamus Banaghan was up behind the goals running up and down and shouting encouragement at Terry who was as solid as a wall. There were two points in it to Carrickmore when a goal from The Kilmacden forward put them a point ahead. The Carrickmore team were incensed as victory seemed to be slipping away, there was thirty seconds left and they had the ball, they were going to go for a goal. Almost the entire squad headed for the Kilmacaden Goal mouth, Tom looked on his heart in his mouth as he squinted up in the sunlight at Terry who seemed to have shrunk, Seamus Banaghan was behind Terry, Shouting keep calm Terry, you can do

152

it as it seemed to Terence that the whole field were thundering up towards him. He gulped, but held steady as the presence of Seamus seemed to give him confidence, he squared his shoulders as the ball came up to the goals and with his heart in his mouth he caught the ball. The referee blew the final whistle they had won. Seamus Banaghan jumped on top of Terry almost knocking the wind out of him, I knew you were going to be the best goalie ever he said as the rest of the team came tearing up amid screams of joy and laughter. The Cup was presented to the team and George came over with his box camera to record the win for posterity. Tom Sheehan also came over and clapped Terry on the back, Well done son was all he said as he knew he would have disgraced himself by bursting into tears if he said any more. Sally also knew enough to just shake hands with Terry, she would save the hugs for later. Lily and Kate just waved they would also save hugs for later. Frank and Jane were back on the lorry and playing a selection of tunes to entertain the crowd as the children excitedly sat on the grass in front of the Punch and Judy show. Mary, Sally and a reluctant Lizzie were heading over to Madame Zelda. Two young girls came out giggling from the caravan. Will we go in together or on our own asked Mary, I don't want to go in at all muttered Lizzie, that decided it for Mary come on she said linking their arms, together it is, one for all and all for one as like the three musketeers they made their way into the darkness of the caravan. Madame Zelda could be any age in the gloom of the caravan, she had a red bandana around her head from which medals

153

jingled as she moved, there was a round table with a crystal ball in the middle and Lizzie thought it was quite spooky. Sit down one at a time please and cross my palm with silver. Mary went first as Lizzie and Sally stood to one side, she placed the shilling in Madame's palm which she quickly took and placed it in a tin box beside her chair. You have been over the water my dear but you will be staying put from now on. Mary nodded but said nothing, you have a child who will bring you much happiness and I see another child who has not arrived yet, Mary gasped there was no way that this gypsy could have known about the baby. You will receive a very important letter in the next few weeks, that is all, the crystal is clouding over. Sally was next as she greased the gypsy's palm with silver, she thought there isn't much that she can tell me that I don't already know. Your life is going to change very soon, expect it to be very different than what you are used to. Sally looked at her in alarm, don't worry my dear said the Gypsy it's for the best. You will come into some money from an unexpected source, the crystal is fading again, Sally got up and The reluctant Lizzie sat down, The gypsy was so long looking into the ball that they thought she had forgotten they were there. Ah she said I just had a visitation from someone who has passed, someone close to you, all three women were shocked. He says you are to be happy and that he will always watch over you. Your destiny awaits you be careful you do not miss it. The gypsy lay back, that is all, I am tired now you may go. The three women came out blinking into the sunshine each of them absorbed in what they

154

had just been told. Do you really believe her asked Sally looking at the other two, but she knew as she asked that they did.

Chapter Fifteen

Pat Quinn didn't enjoy the boat trip from Kingstown to Holyhead. He wasn't on for talking to anyone, he had too much on his mind. He had checked in the tin trunk that his mother kept every letter that she had ever got. He was careful not to ruffle them up too much as he knew she often went through them. He found a bundle of Mary's letters and spotted the address of St. Bernard's Convent in Windsor, he also wrote down the address of the house where Mary, George and Kate had lived. He knew Molly had a cousin in the Convent where the girls had gone on their holidays all those years ago. He had the money that Dan had sent him stuffed in his wallet and a change of clothes in an old leather bag that belonged to his grandfather. He left the key of the house under the flower pot at the back door for Jim Collins and headed off with not much of a clue as to what he was going to do. He Slept for most of the long train journey from Holyhead to London and was awoken by the porter shouting, carriage doors banging and people rushing everywhere. Pat had never seen anything like it, the noise level was deafening. He staggered out on to the platform holding on to his bag as the crowds swirled and shoved around him. He went over to a porter and asked him how he could get to Windsor and after getting directions with some difficulty as he didn't understand the accent he was finally on the way. It was only a twenty minute journey and Pat was relieved as they came into the Station. He decided that he would find somewhere to stay for the few days and then he would try and locate Molly. The high street was full of shoppers and Pat had enough sense to know that there would be nowhere to stay on this street. He kept going on to the next street, Burlington Avenue it said on a little plaque, Pat kept walking until he spotted a sign, Kent House, Respectable rooms, board and lodging. He headed up the steps and entered a hallway with a desk in front of him. A tall man was writing in a ledger, Good afternoon he said to Pat, Pat nodded and asked if he could have a room with breakfast for the next four days. Certainly my man, is that an Irish accent I hear, it is indeed said Pat warily. My Great grandfather came from Co. Cork said the man. John O Donovan is the name he said sticking out his hand to Pat, and Pat immediately felt at home. He was shown to a nice room with everything he needed and the bathroom was just next door. He was anxious to get started on his quest to find Molly and didn't bother unpacking as he locked his room and headed out once more on to the street. He asked a few people where St. Bernard's Convent was with no results and wished that he had thought to ask John O Donovan, however just as he was beginning to despair he suddenly saw a sign saying St. Bernard's Primary and Secondary schools ahead, the Convent must be nearby. He kept walking until suddenly there it was With his heart in his mouth he entered the gates and went up the avenue and approached the large front door. The Bell was on the right and as he pushed it he felt he might faint, Pat Quinn who had never even had a cold was going to faint. He pulled himself together as footsteps could be heard, the door opened and a young Nun looked out at him, Can I help you she asked softly, I am looking for Sister Bernadette please said Pat in a voice so unlike his own, that he had to cough quickly to cover his panic. I 'm afraid some of the Sisters are gone on Retreat this week the young Nun said and I think Sister Bernadette is one of them. Please come into the visitor's parlour and I will get Reverend Mother and she will be able to tell you more. Pat stood in the pristine parlour waiting for the Reverend Mother, he had no clue in his head as to what he was going to do next if Sister Bernadette was gone on retreat, but he would cross that bridge when he came to it. He was in England and Maybe Molly was still somewhere near here. The door opened so quietly that the elderly Nun was almost beside him before he heard her. The young postulant had told her that there was a gentleman from Ireland in the parlour looking for Sister Bernadette. Mother Agnes looked at the young man standing awkwardly in the sunshine that was beaming in the Convent window, It shone on his auburn curls as if making a halo around his head and he turned around to greet her she knew instinctively who he reminded her of. She softly told him to sit down as she rang the bell for the postulant to bring them tea and sandwiches, she knew this would be a difficult conversation. I was hoping to see Sister Bernadette, Pat sad after shaking the Reverend Mothers hand. That is too bad she stated Most of our senior sisters are gone on retreat this week including Bernadette, but maybe I can help you she said giving him an opening if he needed one. Pat made up his mind that he liked this elderly Lady and he asked her if she remembered the visit of his sister Mary and her friend Molly coming to stay in the Convent with Molly's cousin over a decade ago. Indeed, I remember them well she smiled as the tea tray arrived with an inviting array of dainty sandwiches, neither of them said anything as the young postulant poured them a cup of tea. Pat who by now was really hungry gulped down several sandwiches and let the strong tea trickle down his parched throat. I was wondering if you knew where Molly went after she left here Pat muttered not looking directly at the Nun. Mother Agnes, who knew that at that moment Molly was more than likely sitting in her little cottage in the Convent grounds probably making plans with Patrick, the children were on their Summer break for four weeks and Molly and her son would be spending a lot of their days together, she thought for a moment, well she said it would be very unethical of me to divulge the address of someone to a person whose is relatively unknown to me, If you know Molly so well and your sister was her best friend how is it that you don't know where Molly is already. Pat knew he was going to have to tell this Nun his sorry story. He cleared his throat and began, I know you will think a lot less of me when you have heard me out he said, but it the truth is, my sister has no idea that I am here, she probably does know where Molly is but she Won't tell me anything. I did something a long time ago that I am very ashamed of, I took advantage of the young innocent girl that Molly was, he looked at the Reverend mother to see how she was taking this, but her face remained impassive, I have regretted it every day of my life since, I told her to go off and find out about the world and to forget me. I in my wisdom didn't realise how much I loved her and have never stopped loving her. The war started here and the girls were away for years, my sister Mary met an Englishman and they now live back in Ireland with their daughter Kate, It is due mostly to Kate that I am here. I am very fond of my niece and one day a few weeks ago I was giving her a piggy back when she knocked the bottom out of my world by announcing that her cousin Patrick in England looked just like me with hair the same colour, she also mentioned that he lived with her Godmother whom she called Aunty Molly, I put two and two together and I think Patrick is my son. The Reverend Mother looked at him but still said nothing, Pat continued, I had no idea that Molly was having my baby, I would have gone to the ends of the earth to find her if I had known he said earnestly. Mother Agnes believed him. If you know where she went please tell me he pleaded. The old nun thought carefully before she declared, I do know where Molly and Patrick are, but it is not for me to tell you that you can see them, that is entirely up to Molly, you must understand. Pat couldn't believe his ears, she knew where they were, but she wouldn't tell him. I have only four days here and then I must go back to Ireland he said, please for God's sake tell me. Mother Agnes stood up, I can't she said breaking Pats heart, but I will get word to Molly that you are here and she can decide if she wishes to see you or not. Pat had to be satisfied with that even though he wasn't very happy about it. He took out the little card that John O Donovan had given him with the address and Telephone number of Kent house and he gave it to the Nun. Thank you very much Mother he said I will be at this boarding house all day tomorrow and the next day waiting for some sort of message from you. The Nun smiled and bowed out of the room and the postulant appeared to let him out of the Convent. He didn't see the people walking along the street, he didn't notice the beautiful grounds of the convent, he didn't see the woman and boy with the auburn curls entering a side gate into those very grounds. He walked like a blind man back to the boarding house and went upstairs and even though it was early evening he fell exhausted on to the bed and slept all night.

Molly had been on nights and now had five days off. She had walked with Patrick to the school in the morning where he was doing a swimming camp with the boy scouts and gone to early Mass, she was in the habit of going to Mass as often as she could but she hadn't been to confession since she left Ireland. She was relatively happy and knew how lucky she was to be living in the Convent cottage. She was lonely sometimes but work and Patrick kept her busy, but not so busy that she didn't think about Pat Quinn and wishing that she could stop loving him. There was a lovely young doctor at the hospital who had tried several times to take her out but she always declined. Mary seldom mentioned Pat in her weekly letter and she could not bring herself to ask about him. There was a new letter from Ireland on the mat when she got in the door, she would make a cup of tea and sit down to enjoy Mary's letter which was always full of news, news about people that Molly almost felt that she knew. She laughed to herself as she read and visualised Annie Quinn sauntering around in a pair of toeless sandals, she was delighted that Kate had taken to the Irish dancing so well, she also felt as if she knew Mary's friends Sally and Lizzie and she enjoyed the news of their visit to Madame Zelda. Mary had kept the best bit of news until the end of the letter. Yourself and Patrick have to come over in February when Baby Hill number two will be making an entry into the world. I insist, my mother got over me marrying a protestant and I'm sure she would be over the moon to have Patrick in her life, surely your parents too would love to meet their only grandchild. Times are changing here Molly and things that wouldn't have been acceptable ten years ago are now becoming a way of life. Please don't say no straight away think about it. Molly was delighted for Mary and George but she noticed Mary never mentioned Pat in the letter. Molly sat at the table thinking about Patrick and how different his life would be with four loving grandparents in it, His Aunt Mary, uncle George and his cousin Kate and the new baby. He had plagued her to go to Ireland after they had left, He constantly mentioned them and how much he missed them. Of late he was growing up he was now ten and had few friends, just the boys at school, Molly was very strict and kept him mostly about the Convent, she knew this couldn't last for ever and that he would want to spread his wings. She hated the fact that he was growing up in England and often visualised both of

162

them running through the meadows back home. She was about to read Mary's letter again when there was a knock at the door. Molly rarely had visitors apart from one of the Sisters or Mrs Lydon from the boarding house where Patrick was born, she warily went to open the door gasped in shock when she saw Mother Agnes standing there, What's wrong Mother she gulped, is it Patrick. Mother Agnes shook her head, no my child Patrick is fine, may I come in? Molly stumbled back, thoughts flying through her mind, it must be about the cottage she thought, even though the convent gardener lived in Windsor and came in every day maybe he wanted to be closer, what would they do, where would they go, all of these thoughts crossed her mind as she hastily invited the Mother in to sit down. I will put the kettle on she said as she went to plug it in, it was still warm from her own cup of tea but when Mother nodded her head and sat down Molly knew it was something serious as the elderly Nun seldom left her rooms these days and she certainly never left the convent. She sat down and waited for the Nun to speak. Molly my dear child, I had a visitor yesterday, A very distraught young man from Ireland called Pat Quinn, A young man who in my estimation looks very like his son. Molly went white and became speechless, As she gulped for air Mother continued, he asked me if I knew where you were and as I couldn't tell him I lie, I told him that I did but that it was not up to me as to whether you wanted to meet him or not. He is here in England for the next couple of days and staying at this address the nun stated putting the card that Pat had given her on the table. He knew nothing of Patrick and said that if he did he would have been over after you on the next boat, it was something that his little niece Kate said that aroused his suspicions. Now Molly, the Reverend mother said kindly I want you to think long and hard before you decide what to do. Remember the story I told you about my sister Agnes and her situation and how I never saw her again. I do not know if she is alive or dead, I do not know if she had a girl or a boy, that child is my nephew or niece but we will never know each other. Please remember all of this when you are making your decision. The Mother stood up to leave, I am always there for you whatever you decide. A shocked Molly saw her to the door and went back into the kitchen where she sat down before her legs gave way. What was she to do, Pat was here, she had the card in her hand with the number of the boarding house. It was now twelve O 'Clock, Patrick stayed in the swimming camp for lunch and wouldn't be back until Three thirty. She would have to talk to him after all he had come all this way once he had found out that they had a child. She owed him that much. She knew where Kent house was she had often passed it on her way to the high street. She made up her mind before she lost her nerve, she would go over there this minute and get it over with.

Molly went in the door of Kent house just as John O' Donovan was coming downstairs, I am sorry my dear he said we are fully booked up this week, I can let you have the name of an other boarding house if you wish. Sally told him that she didn't need a room, but that she wished to speak to one of his guests, a Mr Pat Quinn, she stumbled over the name that she muttered in her sleep, the name that was never out of her mind. He looked at her strangely and asked if Mr Quinn was expecting her as he carefully took in her appearance. She looked a bit distraught he decided and was unsure as to whether Mr Pat Quinn would want to see her. Just wait in the recreation room to your right he said and I will go and see if Mr Quinn is in his room. Molly went into the room on legs as weak as water, she sat down on a sofa with a plop and wiped her face on the sleeve of her coat, was she mad to be coming here maybe she should have left things the way they were, what would she tell her son, She stood up with a start and decided to run and leave before the landlord came back. She ran out of the room as if the Devil was after her straight into the arms of Pat Quinn. Ten years of longing, loneliness, and hopelessness all the pent of years of emotion, came to a head as Molly burst into tears, Pat held her in his arms while trying to get his handkerchief out of his jacket pocket, he looked over Molly's head at John Donovan who was coming down the stairs, John took in the situation at a glance and bundled them back into the recreation room, you Won't be disturbed in here he said as most of my guests are out for the day. He closed the door and went back to his desk vowing to keep an eye out in case they were disturbed. As Molly hiccupped and cried, Pat murmured endearments, My darling Molly, Why didn't you tell me you were having my child, why did Mary not tell me, I would have followed you. I loved you then and I love you now. All of the things that

Molly so often dreamed to hear Pat Quinn saying were being said. Pat's shirt was by now soaking wet with all the tears that came out of Molly, eventually she calmed down, as Pat led her over to the sofa, still keeping his arm around her, I swore Mary to secrecy it was enough that I had to be in disgrace, but I wasn't sure if you would want to know, you told me to go and find someone else but there never was and never will be anyone else she hiccupped. Pat cursed himself for ever having gone into that hayshed. We can fix this he said, I want to marry you, I want to meet my son and get to know him, please Molly we can go home, it will only be a one day wonder he said repeating Jim Collins's words. Can you imagine your mother 's face if you landed home with a readymade family Molly gulped she could almost feel Annie Quinn's wrath from there. What about my parents, I write to my father every now and then, my mother is gone into some sort of decline and doesn't even know where she is, never mind where I am, I pretend to my father that I am busy studying, I get my letters sent to the post office in Windsor so he Won't follow me over. Pat pleaded with Molly to no avail, I can't go back Father Murphy would be on the doorstep as soon as I'd land. Pat looked at her sadly, what can I do I can't let you go again. Neither of them thought about Pat staying in England as they both knew it was impossible for him to leave his home and parents, the shock would kill them. I have to go back to my house at the Convent now Molly said Patrick will soon be home. You called him after me said Pat playing on her sympathy, Indeed, I did not she said with a look of the old Molly about her. He was born on St Patrick's day what else could I call him. I will tell him about you this evening and you can come over and meet him tomorrow. I live in the Convent grounds and there is always a sister walking around who will point you in the right direction. Come at three O 'clock, Patrick is finished his swimming lessons by then and we will talk. Pat had to be satisfied with that, but before she left he kissed her gently on the mouth. He knew he would have to find a solution as the kiss progressed into anything but gentle. He pulled away reluctantly, go on so and I will see you tomorrow. John O'Donovan relaxed when he saw Molly coming out of the room with a totally different look on her face. Thank you she said as she left, He waited until Pat came out and he saw a changed man. He said nothing only continued on at his books as Pat went back up to his room.

Molly Was so happy that she nearly skipped back to her house, but she came down to earth when she realised that there really was no solution to the problem. She had to think about what she was going to tell Patrick about his father. She really wanted to get married but how could she ever go back and face everyone at home. Then she thought long and hard about what Mother Agnes had said to her as she came in the Convent side gate. Patrick came in ten minutes after her, his auburn curls still damp from the pool. She was so lucky because he still was the sunny happy boy that the convent had reared, He carefully hung his wet swimsuit on the clothes line as she followed him out into the garden, Sit down Patrick she said pulling out two of the wooden garden chairs for them to sit on, he looked at his mother's serious face, is there something wrong mum he asked, am I in trouble.

Molly took a deep breath, I have never told you anything about your father she gulped, Patrick looked at her and asked is he dead. No he is not dead, he is very much alive, he lives in Ireland with your grandparents. The look of joy on Patrick's face was something that Molly would never forget. I have a father, I have grandparents he shouted jumping up and knocking over his chair as he rushed at her to hug her. Molly was astonished Yes you have son, she said carefully and your Auntie Mary is really your Aunt, your father is her brother. Patrick looked at her in disbelief, but mum why did you never tell me this, do they not want me he said sitting down on the side of the upturned chair with a shocked look on his face. Molly couldn't bear it she ran to him, putting her arms around him. I am so sorry, Your grandparents don't know anything about you, you have your fathers parents and you also have two grandparents on my side, my father and mother who are also your grandparents. They all live in Ireland. Then why are we here he said reasonably. Molly took another deep breadth, well before you were born Myself and Aunty Mary came over to England on holiday, but just before we were due to go back the war started and we couldn't travel. You were born here and then I did my nursing training and it never seemed the right time to go back. I didn't tell anyone about you and your father didn't know or he would have been over straight away she said repeating what Pat had told her. She wondered how much of this made sense to his ten year old mind, Before he could ask her anything else she told him that his daddy was in Windsor and wanted to meet him. His green eyes so like his father's shone with pure joy, Molly couldn't help but laugh even though her heart was in her mouth at the thought of the outcome of the visit, she also knew it was up to her as to which path she took. She could stay in England and be miserable for the rest of her life or she could face the wrath of Kilmacaden. Patrick was up at the crack of dawn the next day, he came into her room as she tried to struggle up, she had been awake for half the night tossing and turning and had fallen asleep just as the dawn broke it seemed like she was asleep for five minutes when her son came bounding in dressed in his School uniform. She looked at him in surprise why are you wearing your uniform she asked bewilderedly, I think its very smart and I look very grown up in it, I want to look my best when I'meet my father he replied. Molly sat up and nodded at him, you look wonderful and your dad will be very proud of you she said as she rubbed the sleep out of her eyes but are you not going swimming first, No Mummy I don't want to go swimming, I want to stay here in case he comes early.Molly decided to let it go, all right so she said but go on off with you now until I get dressed and we will have breakfast together before he comes. Patrick obediently left Molly as she decided what she was going to wear for the biggest day of her son's life.

Chapter Sixteen

Pat Quinn was eating his breakfast in Kent house as he impatiently looked at the clock over the mantlepiece in the dining room, he might have well have been eating sawdust as his mind was totally taken up with the thoughts of seeing Molly again and meeting his son for the first time. He thought that three o'clock was too long to wait and decided that as soon as he was finished he was going to head over to St. Bernard's. He reached the Convent at the same time as a priest who was opening the gates into the Avenue. Good morning are you going in Father Horton said to the young man who seemed to be undecided whether he was going in or coming out. Pat looked at the priest excuse me Father, I am just going in but I think I'm a bit early, Sure Mass in the Convent is in half an hour are you going to that, you can be in with me said the priest. Pat stuttered a bit well I'm actually going to see Molly Mc Gee, she lives in the grounds somewhere. She does indeed said Father Horton who like Mother Agnes immediately saw the resemblance to young Patrick Mc Gee, whom he had baptised and given his First Communion, is she expecting you he asked, yes she is said Patrick warily, was this priest going to forbid him to see Molly. Well then he said I will walk down to the Cottage along with you, I have a bit of time before Mass. This didn't really suit Pat who would much rather be going on his own, but he kept his council and said thank you as they walked between the shrubs on along the way. You are over from Ireland obviously said the priest as the silent Patrick couldn't think of anything to say but he did answer with a muffled yes Father. Did you know Molly over there he baited Pat, Pat was beginning to wish that he had waited until three o' Clock like Molly had asked him to, Yes Father he said again. Suddenly as they came into view of the cottage a boy in a school uniform came bounding up, Good morning Father Horton he said and turning to Pat he said Are you my father? The priest looked at the two of them as they stood staring at each other, Pat was so choked up at the love that came out of him for his son, that he could only nod as the boy rushed up and locked his arms around his knees, I've always known you would come someday even though my mummy never mentioned you and as Pat listened to his son's beautiful clipped English, he thought he sounded more like George Hill's son than his own. Father Horton was strangely moved as he gently asked Patrick where his mummy was, she wasn't ready when I came out she said my daddy was coming at Three but I got ready ages ago in case my Father came early, and right you were said Father Horton, Why don't you show your daddy around the orchard and gardens and I will go in and tell your mum where you are. Patrick put his hand trustingly into Pat's as they walked away from the priest towards the orchard.

Molly was just coming down stairs when there was a tap on the door, she thought it couldn't possibly be Pat as it was too early, She stood back in shock as Father Horton came through the door, good morning Molly he said I have just left Patrick and his father up at the orchard, Molly's mouth fell open, what did you say Father she stammered, I think you heard me Molly the priest smiled, There is no denying the relationship between those two peas in a pod. Father I am so sorry, I am not married to Patrick's father, that is why I have never been to Confession since I left Ireland, that is why I left Ireland, but Patrick's father didn't know any of this and as soon as he found out he came over and now he wants to marry me, but you know and I know that I can never go back. The priest looked hard at her and said I don't have much time Molly as Mass is in fifteen minutes, but kneel down her right now and we will do confession. She looked at him once more with her mouth open as she obediently knelt down. You have just confessed to me he said, I give you absolution. You may say a decade of the Rosary for your penance and now I really must go. There is a solution to every problem he said as he went out the door and I want you to know that I am also very good at the sacrament of Marriage. God Bless you Molly.

Molly pinched herself to see if she was dreaming, she had been absolved of her sin, she was as free as a bird, she could go back to Confession and she promised herself that there never would be a sin on her soul again, well maybe just little ones she laughed to herself suddenly feeling as giddy as a the young girl that had danced all those years ago in the village hall. Father Horton's last words rang in her head, I am also very good at the Sacrament of Marriage.

Chapter Seventeen

Tom Sheehan was looking at Sally with a total look of disbelief on his face. They were sitting in the kitchen after the children had gone to bed, Christy was fed and also down for the night. They had been sitting at the table for the past hour while Tom still sat in disbelief at his wife's news. She had been to her father's to bring over his washing as she did every week. Tim Carey was in his eighties, he had refused to come in to the village and live with Tom And Sally when they had asked him after Sally's mother had died. He knew they were short of space and he liked living on the farm where he had been born and raised. He didn't keep cattle anymore, just the one cow for milking and a few hens for the eggs. He had no son just the three daughters, Sally and her two sisters, both living in America. The farmhouse was big and roomy with four bedrooms a box room and the wonderful new bathroom that he had installed when the electricity came. Downstairs there was a big kitchen, a scullery a back room and a parlour that Tim had never used since his wife's funeral. He loved Sally and Tom and his grandchildren with a passion and appreciated the fact that Sally took his washing over to her house each week and he was a part of all their special celebrations. He also knew that her time was stretched between the five children, the shop Tom and himself. They both worked hard, but they always seemed in a pinch for money. Neither Tom nor Sally ever mentioned any of this to Tim but he knew from conversations with his grandchildren that things were tight. He also knew that Tom kept the shop open until all hours hoping to catch a stray shilling or two. He had made up his mind last week and had gone into the solicitor's office in town and signed over the farm the house and contents to Sally with one condition, that he be allowed to spend the rest of his days there. Sally was gobsmacked when she went over with his clean washing and he presented her with the deeds and his will. What about Eileen and Norah in America she argued, Tim laughed sure those two don't even remember where they were born. Sally knew this was true so she said no more The first thing that came into her mind was Madame Zelda's prediction that her life would change. Dad are you sure you want to do this she asked when she got her breath back. I never was more sure of anything Tim stated, you are the best daughter a man could have, if you can persuade Tom and the children to come and live here I will be the happiest man alive, but even if you don't and it is for you to decide, it is all yours take it with my blessing. Sally jumped up and flung her arms around her father who took all this hugging with much embarrassment. Go on out of that he said and tell your husband and see what he says. Oh and by the way I have a bit of money put by for you so you can do up the house any way you want. Sally had related all of this to Tom when they had at last got the place to themselves. Just imagine Tom she said the girls could have a bedroom, the boys could have a bedroom we could have a bedroom all to ourselves. There is a bathroom and I wouldn't have to be traipsing out there to look after my father. Tom looked at her, you have forgotten something important he said looking hurt, Sally looked at him, my shop, what would happen to my shop. Sally thought long and hard, She hated the shop and the way it hung around their neck never giving them more than a few days off each year, always stopping them from doing anything together. She suddenly came up with a solution. You can come over to the shop each day at nine o'clock and close at six in the evenings like they do in most civilised shops she added looking at him from under her eyebrows. Tom said nothing if truth be told he too was tired of the long days in the shop, he wanted to be able to go up to the pitch with Terry, he wanted to be able to have dinner with his wife as well as his children, he wanted to have Sunday's off so he could go to Mass with everyone else and not have to stay and meet the paper delivery and then leave Sally minding the shop while he ate his breakfast. He thought about Tim Carey's farm and the big roomy house, he had never been a farmer as his father had worked on the roads for the County Council and they never had any land. He had worked as a shop boy in Town and saved every halfpenny to get the money together for the shop. He knew they were cramped with Terry and the baby in their bedroom and the girls all crowded into the other small bedroom. He looked up at Sally, she never complained even though he knew she was tired all the time, do you think I have got the makings of a farmer in me was all he said. Sally jumped up she knew the battle was won, I think Tom Sheehan that you will be the best Farmer ever.

Mary was tidying the breakfast dishes when she heard Sally come tearing in through the back door, she skidded to a halt when she saw George sitting at the kitchen table. Oh I am sorry she said I thought you'd be at work, George laughed, well I can always make myself scarce if you want me to. Sally quickly apologised, no You might as well hear my important news as I am just bursting to tell anyone who will listen. Mary plugged in the kettle, sit down so and I 'll make some tea for us and a cup of coffee for George. That gypsy was so right about my fortune Sally said, my father is after giving me and Tom the farm, the house and money to do it up remember she said that my life would change and that I would come into money, well there you go its all happened. Mary got up to hug her friend, that is great, I am delighted for you all. George ever practical said mildly, but what about the shop will you still keep it on. Well Sally said, We are not sure what to do, I suggested to Tom that we just have certain opening hours so that we could have more time together, he is thinking hard about it you see he has never lived on a farm but Tom is always willing to learn and the children will be over the moon to have new bedrooms and a bathroom and not to be living over the shop, it's like a dream. George and Mary laughed at this new and girlish Sally who seemed to have got younger as her troubles were fast disappearing. George looked over the figures he was studying at the table and came to a decision, I might have a solution he said, I am on the lookout for a building in the village for a store house for my firm, I wonder would Tom consider selling me the property, it would be ideal and Tom could concentrate on his new career of farming. All three of them laughed at that but Sally couldn't wait to get back to Tom to see what he thought. She threw her arms around Mary and George and said you are the best friends ever, I am going home now to break all this latest news to Tom. Thank you again and she tore out the door faster than she had skidded in.

Lizzie Banaghan was in a bit of a fix. She had the pig ready for killing, it was the one job on the farm that she would not do, she had always got Larry Devine to do it. The bacon was cured afterwards and kept them in meat for twelve months. She hadn't seen Larry since the day of the Parish sports when they had been staring at each other like idiots. She had her hair firmly stuck in a bun on top of her head and she had vowed it was going to remain there. She also knew that she looked better with it hanging loose and for some daft reason she felt younger with it down. She thought about Larry and his strong brown arms and how good he was to the children especially Seamus who practically hung out over there every evening hoping that Larry had changed his mind about letting him drive the tractor. Larry was quite firm about it and told Seamus in no uncertain terms that his mother would kill the two of them. Seamus knew that his mother had been furious, but he thought she had got over it as she never mentioned it since. That doesn't matter Larry told the young boy, I gave her my word. Seamus had to make do with that, but he said to Larry, the pig is ready for killing and when you come over maybe we could get at her again. Well young fellow tell your mother I will be over this evening to do the job, but I am not asking her anything, you will have to wait a while until you get a licence. Seamus groaned sure I 'll be ages waiting for that. Go on off home now and I 'll see you around six you can help me with the grishkins when I have the job done.

Lizzie was hanging the washing on the rickety old clothesline at the back of the house when Seamus passed her by on his way in the back door. Larry said to tell you he'll be over around six he muttered, still smarting and annoyed at his mother for stopping him from driving the tractor, Lizzie dropped the clothes pegs with the fright of Seamus words Larry was coming over, Oh good god what was she going to do as she unconsciously tightened her bun on top of her head. She left the clothes on the ground and ran in after Seamus, what do you mean Larry is coming over she asked looking at him with a frown, He's coming to kill the pig of course said Seamus what did you think he was coming over for. What indeed thought Lizzie with a feeling of disappointment that shocked her. What is the matter with me she thought rushing out again to hang the rest of the clothes on the line. She got everything ready in a frenzy, the big dish to catch the blood, out of which she made black pudding. Larry always brought his own knife and the children later blew up the pig's blather to make a football out of it. She always made Tea for Larry when the mission was accomplished. She couldn't change that or the children would be wondering and thinking something was wrong. She would keep things exactly as she had done in the past

178

she decided as she gave out to herself for being such a goose. She set the table in the kitchen and sat there like a nervous wreck. Sean came in throwing his wellingtons behind the door. Can I have my tea early this evening I am going down to Terry Sheehan's house. Terry's mam is looking after the shop and his dad is going to bring us up to the pitch. Lizzie agreed to give him something to eat and to let him go even though she wanted them all about her this evening. All right you can go she said but be back here before dark. He was no sooner gone than Lily came rushing in Mam can I go to Kate's house please, Mrs Hill asked me to come to tea and she said she would bring me back home. We think that Sooty is not a boy cat anymore but a girl cat and Kate thinks she might be having kittens. Lizzie felt like her household was falling apart, but her children had all their jobs done about the farm and she had no excuse not to let them go, at least Seamus would be here she thought as she tightened her hair in its bun into extreme distress, she could feel the roots pulling at her forehead so she loosened it a little, her face flushed with dread, fear and excitement.

Larry Devine was getting ready to go over to Banaghan's to kill the pig. He had done it every year since Denis had died. He knew Lizzie would have the tea ready for him and he didn't know how he was going to go in there and eat. He had thought of Lizzie every day since she had beaten the head off him, she was in his thoughts when he was milking and when he was doing all the other jobs around the farmyard. He had never even looked at a woman before this. His parents were both old when he was born and he had spent most of his adult life caring for them. He was on his own for the past number of years since they had died within a month of each other. When Denis Banaghan passed away he and every other neighbouring farmer had rowed in to help Lizzie and the children. He had got very fond of the children as they often came over to him in the evening. He had never really looked at Lizzie until that eventful day on the tractor and now she was never out of his head. He knew he had it bad, he also knew he hadn't a clue what to do about it. Lizzie was beautiful she could have her pick of any man but she had never looked at anyone since Denis, at least he had never heard of her going out with anyone. He wouldn't even know how to ask her out even if he ever got the courage to do so. He was a hopeless case, he thought to himself as he walked over the adjoining field into the Banaghan's yard. Lizzie heard him calling to Seamus to come out to help him, There was no reply to his plea so she went to the bottom of the stairs and called out to her still sulking son. He came down the stairs slowly looking at his mother with a face like a thundercloud. What is the matter with you Seamus she said to her son who was never in bad humour, I don't know why you Won't let me drive Larry's tractor around the bull's field he said, it's quite safe and Larry is always with me and besides it will be good practice for when I buy a tractor myself. Lily laughed in spite of herself, Well now she said, in control once more, when you have the money saved for the tractor I will reconsider letting you practice your driving skills. Seamus knew and so did his mother that this would be never. He went out to Larry and told him his tale of woe. Sure you go and do well at school Seamus, get yourself a good job and you can save up for a tractor although I bet by then it's more like a motor car you'll be wanting. Seamus was in cloud cuckoo land as he held the squealing pig down for Larry. He was dreaming about having a motor car like George Hill, he would bring his mother for drives to the seaside, he would have sunglasses also like George Hill. Larry let a roar at him to get the dish for the blood and his dream bubble burst with a bang. He was a great lad thought Larry as they worked together getting the two sides of bacon ready for salting in the barrel of brine in the scullery. Lizzie had a pan' of hot water ready for them when they went in to get washed up before the tea. Seamus was starving and ate his tea of rasher sausage and egg as if it was the last bit he was ever going to get. He stuffed a bit of his mother's homemade brown bread in his mouth and jumped up from the table, where do you think you are going Lizzie asked the thought of being on her own with Larry being too much for her. Please mam I' m just going up to the pitch, Sean Terry and all the lads are up there, everything is done here, isn't it Larry. Indeed it is said Larry, you were a great help I couldn't have done it without you. Lizzie was beaten, go on so she said be back before dark. Thanks mam he said running out the door leaving Larry and Lizzie sitting opposite each other at the kitchen table. The silence was deafening, they both started to talk at once. That was a fine pig said Larry, was there much bother this evening said Lizzie, they looked at each other and laughed, suddenly it seemed to be all right, the two of them sitting having their tea. I seldom get the place to myself like this Lizzie said filling up Larry's cup of tea once more, Sure you'd need a bit of peace now and then he said, tis too much peace I have myself except when Seamus and Sean come over and keep me entertained. Talking about Seamus Lizzie said, I do not want him driving that tractor and I am serious about what I said that evening. I am serious about what I said that evening too said Larry getting up and going around the table to her with courage coming out of somewhere. I meant what I said about your hair being lovely Lizzie, I think you're lovely too as well as your hair he said hastily, She was totally stuck for words and looked at him coming nearer to her. She self-consciously lifted one hand up to the bun on her head as if it was her armour, her other hand went up to her mouth as she chewed her lip. Just as Larry got to her side Mary Hill, together with Lily and Kate came in the back door. The girls were prattling away and kept going on up into Lily's room while Mary stood there looking at the two of them in astonishment as they pulled away from each other. Oh I' m so sorry she said red with embarrassment I will come back for Kate later. No said Larry who was also rather red around the gills at this stage, I am going now anyway. He went to take his jacket from the back of the chair as he said to Lizzie, I 'll be back tomorrow to salt the bacon. Lizzie was so incapable of speech that she just nodded and sat down with a bang at the table. Mary sat down opposite her, well now she said tell me all. Lizzie was immediately on the defensive, there is nothing to tell. He killed the pig, I gave him his tea that's it. Mary laughed well when I came in it looked he was about ready to kiss you. Lizzie lost the will to argue at this stage and quickly said to Mary do you really think he was going to kiss me? well either that or he was going to take your hair down replied her friend. How long has this been going on. I told you there is nothing going on Lizzie said hotly, well would you like there to be something going on she said reasonably, Lizzie's red face said it all. Well said Mary there is nothing stopping you, he likes you, you like him, the kids like him and as Madame Zelda said don't let your destiny go astray. That fortune teller was right about what she told Sally and her life changing news, she was right about me receiving an important letter and she is probably right about you. Lizzie sat lost in a world with Larry Devine in it when her good manners came to the fore. Have a cup of tea and what's all this about and important letter. Well said Mary it's a long sad story and I don't know if there is going to be a happy ending. I have to tell someone though, I have told George of course but he is no help its always black or white with him. She proceeded to tell Lizzie the saga of herself and Molly up until the time that she herself came back home to Ireland and then she said on the day of the first Communion remember my parents and my brother Pat were there, well somehow or other Kate gave the game away, Pat asked me about Molly a few times but I was under oath from her not to tell him anything and as George always said it would have been the right thing to do anyhow as Pat had a right to know about his son. Anyway when my parents came up for the few weeks at the time of the sports Pat took off for England and found them. He has asked Molly to marry him and come back to the village of Dufflin beside where my family home is. Molly's father was the local Doctor and he still keeps on their family home. You know back then what the Clergy and the older generation were like, Molly would have been disgraced and or disowned by most people. Pat would also have been in the doghouse, but most fellows in that situation got off scot free while the poor girls were treated like outcasts. If they come back my mother will probably have a nervous breakdown, Father Murphy will denounce them from the Altar, Doctor Mc Gee will kill Pat and God knows what else. My father will probably be the only sane one around the place. Its so sad, Patrick their son is over the moon about everything and is longing to come and meet his grandparents and of course to see Kate, myself and George, he is a lovely boy and the image down of Pat. Oh my goodness said Lizzie, thinking to herself how simple her own dilemma was compared to Mary's, Her children loved Larry, he was such a good man and she was a free agent, All of these thoughts were going around in her head when she realised Mary was waiting for an answer of some sort. Well if you ask me I think they should come back times are changing and it will be forgotten in a week or two. There are enough unhappy people in the World and if happiness comes their way they should take it She was including herself in this conversation and Mary knew it. She got up and put her arms around Lizzie, thank you for listening and for your advice which I hope that you to will take yourself too she said smiling at her friend. Lizzie's reply was to put up her hand and pull her hair out of its confinement and let it swing loose, she said nothing but called to the girls to come down. You go home and write to your friend, tell her to marry your brother and to come back and grab what happiness she can. Pat had written to Mary some days after she had received Molly's letter, he wanted her to come home for a few days to back him up while the news was broken to their parents. He would tell their father, while he hoped Mary would break the news to their mother. He was going back to England in a few weeks, Father Horton was going to marry himself and Molly and then he was going to bring his wife and son home to Ireland.

Chapter Eighteen

Molly was packing her clothes in one case and Patrick's in another, she had written to her father and told him everything. She told him she was getting married and coming back home, she said she was sorry for everything and she put her proper address on the top of the letter. She hoped that he would forgive her and understand. She had written some days ago and was hoping that he would at least send her a reply. She heard the knock on the door as she was putting her nurses' uniform in to the case, she wondered would she ever wear it again, Patrick she shouted please answer the door its Mrs Lydon she is coming over to say goodbye. She heard Patrick pounding down the stairs and she heard the deep tones of a man's voice as she tried to fasten the lock on her case. It must be Father Horton she thought as she went down stairs but the sight that met her eyes took her breath away, Her father was sitting on the sofa, tears streaming down his face with his arm around a beaming Patrick, he stood up, as she skidded to a halt at the door oh Molly my darling daughter was all he said as he folded her into his arms.

Pat was a nervous wreck, He had asked Mary to come for a few days to soften up his mother, he knew his father would come round fairly quickly but he had no idea what his mother would do. She always took things so personally, especially things that might upset the neighbours, Father Murphy or the general public and this would be a bitter pill for her to swallow. Mary, George and Kate were coming this evening and tomorrow George was going to take Kate fishing in the small stream down behind the paddock, he had bamboo sticks with twine and hooks ready for them and a jar full of worms wriggling in some clay. He hoped that Mary had a plan as his mind was totally blank. He could hear his mother lighting the fire in the parlour as she always did when she knew that George was coming, she felt she owed it to him to have the best room ready since she had slighted him when she found out that he was a protestant, she realised that he was a good man and that Mary was happy and would never want for anything. She had forgiven him.

Mary was also thinking about what she would say to her mother about Molly and Patrick, George had been no help whatsoever, he couldn't for the life of him see what the problem was, Pat was a grown man for heaven's sake he didn't know about the child and as soon as he did he was doing the right thing. He knew his mother-in-law was a bit of a stickler for "the right thing" so what was the problem. He tried to be sympathetic but failed, himself and Kate would go fishing and take a picnic down to the stream and he would look for the white smoke before he came back.

The Quinns were delighted to welcome the Hill family and Annie was out the door as soon as the car pulled up.Kate jumped into her granny's arms and hugged her much to Annie's delight. I love you granny and I love coming down here, where are granddad and uncle Pat, she chatted on telling Annie that her kitten was now a cat and not a boy at all but a girl cat and that she might be having kittens. Mary muttered under her breath, that's not going to happen for they had the cat neutered some time ago. George said he could have had his appendix out for the price Vet Daly had charged them but Mary knew that it was very tricky for him as he was used to big animals like cows and bulls, neutering cats was more or less unheard of. Kate thought that the cat got a pain in its tummy and had to get medicine to make it better, anyway there would be no kittens. Come on in the tea is ready Annie bustled them all into the parlour, where the turf fire was roaring up the chimney even though it was early September and the sun was cracking the stones outside. I don't want you getting a chill Mary, you know you have to look after yourself for the next few months. I 'm fine mam Mary said sitting as far away from the fire as she could get. I am so happy that you are all here for the weekend Annie continued, I love having you and Kate is such a dote, Won't it be great when there is another grandchild to join her. Mary kicked George under the table in case he put his foot in it as he was liable to say just what he thought. He would never understand the ins and outs of what was acceptable and what wasn't. He got the message and kept his mouth firmly shut. The next morning Kate was up bright and early and as she followed Pat around the yard as he fed the hens and mucked out the cows she talked away to him. Pat's head was a million miles away as he thought about Molly and his son. How would Patrick adjust to life on an Irish farm, Kate seemed to have had no bother and her English accent had all but disappeared. Would he settle into school, how would his mother and Molly get on. He wasn't stupid and he knew that two women in the same house was never going to be easy. Molly insisted she was going to look for a job in the local Hospital as she loved nursing and knew nothing about farming. He wasn't so sure how this would go down at home either as Annie was a firm believer that a mother's place was in the home. God how he wished the weekend was over.

Pat and Mary had decided that when George and Kate had gone fishing that he would talk to his father and Mary would talk to their mother. Pat had a sick feeling in his stomach and didn't eat his breakfast. What's up with you Annie asked as she took his almost full plate back to the sink. I'm just not very hungry today he muttered following his father out to the barn where Paddy was heading just at that moment. Pat looked at his father and said I have something important to tell you, you might be as well to light your pipe and we'll go over and sit on the far wall. Paddy knew his son had been out of sorts lately but he wisely said nothing just took out his pipe and lit up, the smell of the tobacco smoke was somehow comforting to Pat, he associated it with good times when his father was at ease and puffed away on the pipe. Annie didn't like the pipe and Paddy was only allowed an ounce of tobacco every fortnight. He thought he might know why Pat was so nervous, he knew how dull a life his son lived, all he had in the line of excitement was an odd game of cards with Jim Collins or a trip to the races once in a while. He also knew that Dan had sent Pat the fare for America because Meg had written to him privately telling him to let Pat go if he could and that they would look out for him. Neither father nor son ever mentioned the money. Paddy also knew that Pat loved the farm and all of the necessary work that it entailed but he couldn't think of any other reason only that Pat wanted to leave for the U.S.A. He puffed away and waited for his son to speak. Pat took a deep breath, Dad I am leaving to get married, Paddy almost fell off the wall, this was not what he was expecting to hear, he looked at his son in astonishment, but waited to hear the rest. Pat told him everything from the Summer when he was going around on the quiet with Molly Mc Gee until the time he followed her to England. I regret what happened and I had no idea that she was carrying my baby. He is now ten years old and a lovely boy, Molly's priest in the Convent where herself and Mary stayed is going to marry us next week. Doctor Mc Gee is over there with them at the moment. We will be coming back to live here if that is possible. The sky didn't fall as Paddy slowly digested all of the information, He had another grandson, Pat wasn't going to America, everything would be all right. That's grand so son he said putting out his hand to shake Pats, then he thought about Annie and all that she was going to say on the matter, he looked at his son and said how will we tell your mother. Pat who looked as if the weight of the world had been lifted off him send with a hint of the old Pat, I left that to Mary, she is telling mam now.

Well Pat I think we should go down to the stream and join George and Kate until it's safe to go back home.

Mary made tea and took out the apple tart that her mother had made the night before, I was saving that for this evening Annie grumbled as she sat down at the table, she loved the cup of tea and the fact that Mary was here was lovely. Sit down and tell me all the plans you have made for my new grandchild she said taking her cup in her hand. Mary sat down took a deep breath and said Mam I do want to tell you about your grandchild, but not this one she said patting her stomach. Annie looked perplexed is there something wrong with Kate she asked. No Kate is fine. You remember my friend Molly Mc Gee that went to England with me, indeed and I do said Annie and the bould strap never came home, she broke her father's heart and her poor mother is languishing in a nursing home in Dublin. Mary continued as Annie waffled on. Mollie has a ten-year-old son and she is not married and that is why she didn't come home. Annie gasped blessing herself I knew she was a bould one, she spent the summer here before you went to England traipsing around after Pat, Good job he never looked at her or she might have blamed him. Do you know who the father is, Mary took another deep breath, Mam, Pat is the father but he didn't know Molly was having a baby. Annie jumped up knocking over her tea which fell unnoticed as she ranted and raved. Pat would never take advantage of a young girl, I just know he wouldn't. Mary tried to pacify her mother who was by now so agitated that she shredded her apron into rags. Mam he loved Molly but he tried to do the right thing and make her forget him. Annie s face was frightening, by making her have a baby she shouted, no Mam Mary said trying to calm her down, it was only the once and Pat is still regretting it even though at the time he didn't know Molly was pregnant. Kate let it slip on the first Communion day and Pat decided to look for Molly. You knew, Annie spat, Kate knew, I suppose even the protestant knew she roared. Mary knew how bad her mother was taking this when she reverted to calling George ''The Protestant''. Doctor Mc Gee is over there with Molly at the moment Mary said, this was the last straw as far as Annie was concerned, Oh God Bless us all, he'll kill Pat and him not even the father. Mam Mary said gently Pat is the father Molly never so much as looked at anyone only Pat. They are getting married next week and Pat is going to bring his wife and child back here. Over my dead body is she coming in here, Annie sunk into the chair. How am I ever going to leave this house again, what will Father Murphy say, what will the neighbours say she muttered to herself, just leave me alone will you I am going up to bed. Mary 's mouth fell open her mother who never gave into any ailment was taking to the bed, this was bad.

Mary headed for the stream, she knew there was point in trying to make her mother see sense when she was in this mood. Maybe she would change her mind when she saw Patrick and Molly, Mary thought hopefully. She heard the talking long before she got to the stream and arrived just as her father was telling Kate about the time he caught the salmon of Knowledge. She remembered him telling herself and Pat the same yarn. Kate's eyes were round as she listened to her grandfather. She motioned to Pat to come to one side. Mam has taken to the bed she told him quietly and it's not looking good, how did dad take it. Ah you know dad, said Pat he took it all in but didn't say much, he seems ok about it. He didn't give out or anything. I think its best it we leave for Ballybrea this evening replied Mary, I don't want Kate and George to get caught up in this taking to the bed of mam's. Dad is the only one that can talk some sense into her Pat so leave him to get around mam and you keep out of her way. I wish I could go over to England with you for the wedding but I don't want Kate to miss school as she is doing so well but maybe you should come to us when you come back instead of coming home as mam is likely to lock the door. Oh God is it that bad Pat muttered.

The little Chapel in St. Bernards was bathed in sunshine as the congregation of Nuns knelt to watch Patrick Mc Gee wait at the altar with his father Pat Quinn for his mother Molly to come up the Church on the arm of his grandfather Eoin Mc Gee followed by Hannah Lydon who was her matron of honour. Patrick had the rings ready in his pocket and as the two Auburn heads shone in the sunlight no one could deny that this was indeed father and son. Molly looked beautiful in her pink silk dress made by the lightening quick fingers of Sister Winifred and it fitted her slender figure like a glove. She carried a bouquet of pink roses entwined with leaves from the Convent garden. Their happiness was plain to see as Molly's father gave her a kiss on the check and handed her over to Pat Quinn with a smile. Young Patrick beamed as Father Horton pronounced his parents Man and wife. It was a happy day as they all trouped back over to the convent Refectory to partake of the delicious meal provided by the sisters. Molly was overwhelmed, she had to pinch herself a few times to make sure she wasn't dreaming. She was Mrs Pat Quinn and Pat was taking her into his arms to dance as Sister Monica played Danny boy on the rickety old piano. Eoin Mc Gee gallantly took out Hannah Lydon for a waltz around the floor as Patrick and the Sisters looked on in delight. It was a day never to be forgotten even though Molly's mother wasn't there and Pat's family weren't there they both realised that they were a new family unit now united at last. They thanked everyone for the beautiful day of wonderful memories and headed back down to the cottage that had been Molly's home for so long, Patrick walking behind them talking to his grandfather about the school rugby team and the way he could get down into the scrum. Molly took off her pink hat with the lace veil and carefully placed it in to the hatbox that she had borrowed from Mrs Lydon, she shook her black hair loose and Patrick thought he had never seen her so beautiful, his heart was filled with love and sorrow that so much of their lives had been wasted. Molly gazed up at her new husband, she knew instinctively what he was thinking and she squeezed his hand, she looked in surprise at her father as he asked them to sit down as he had something to say to them, you too young Patrick he said as Patrick went to go upstairs. As you know Pat, I spend most of my time in

Dublin just coming to Kilmacden occasionally and then only to air the house in the hope that one day Molly you might come home, Well now is that time, The house is yours and everything in it, I have all that I need in the house in Dublin, I would like to come and visit yourselves and my grandson there from time to time if that's all right. Moly and Pat were astonished, Pat had been thinking how was he going to break the news to Molly about the deadlock at home and now there seemed to be a way out, that is if Molly wanted to live in her old home. One look at her face, eyes shining he knew she was just as happy as him about the news. She ran to get a dog-eared old photo of the house with the surgery to the side out of her bag, a photo that she had taken out and looked at many times, It had seen many a tear fall on it. Look she said to Patrick this is your new home. Eoin Mc Gee took his grandson's hand and said Molly get this boys pyjamas and toothbrush, he is coming to stay in Mrs Lydon's boarding house with me tonight, he will be taking me to see the sights around here tomorrow and we will be back in Lydons about six. Mrs Lydon is treating us all to a fine tea and we will meet you there. I would love if you would let me bring Patrick back to Ireland with me on the day after and himself and myself will get the house aired for you. You can enjoy your few days honeymoon before you come home to Ireland. Patrick who was chomping at the bit to get to His new home was pleading with his mother to let him go. Molly gave in, it would be so nice to have Pat to herself and maybe seeing her father along with Patrick would smooth Annie Quinn's ruffled feathers.

Pat had told her that his mother was not taking the news very well.

Chapter Nineteen

Annie Quinn was still annoyed with Pat and undecided how she was going to deal with the mess as she was calling it, she knew that Mary and George had left early with Kate on the day of the revelation. She was also annoyed with Molly Mc Gee, she was annoyed with Paddy and she was annoyed at the world in general. Paddy had tried to reason with her telling her that Pat knew nothing about the little boy who was their grandchild, that he loved Molly and seemingly had loved her from all those years ago. You do know how unhappy he has been lately, are you going to begrudge him this chance to put things right. Annie argued back, how are we going to present a ten year old grandson to the neighbours, could she not pretend that he is someone else's she ranted. Paddy looked at her shocked to the core, he decided to leave her to sort it out in her own head. He was done, he would wait until the new family came from England and he would deal with it then. He knew that Annie had made no move to get the rooms above stairs ready and he was at his wits end. He decided to go and see Father Murphy who was about the only person in the Parish that would get through to his wife. As he walked through the village with his head down thinking to himself how happy they should all be He was aware of Mrs Corr in the post office banging the window at him. He really didn't want to talk to anyone but she is not the worst he thought to himself as he slowly went into the post office. I was going to wait until the postman came back off his rounds for him to bring this telegram out to you she announced, but then I saw you going by. Paddy knew that she was aware of what was in the envelope that he held in his hand, but he also knew that she was the soul of discretion. Would you like to go into the back room, there is a fire in there, the kettle is boiling, make yourself a cup of tea no one will disturb you and you can read your telegram in peace. Paddy looked at her gratefully, thank you was all he said as he went into the small back room that Mrs Corr took her tea breaks in. He made a good strong mug of tea and thought to himself this is the first bit of peace I have had since Pat broke his news. He opened the brown envelope and took out the piece of paper with trembling hands:

Arriving tomorrow with our grandson Patrick.

Should be there by three o'clock.

Will be staying at my house.

Or I should say Molly and Pat's house as it is now.

Please come over any time.

Molly and Pat arrive on Saturday.

Yours sincerely Eoin Mc Gee.

Paddy sat with the mug of cold tea by his side as he digested this news, so Molly and Pat were probably going to live in the village. It would be very convenient for Pat he mused to himself as it was only minutes away from the farm and Molly would have her own home and not be treading on Annie's toes. It seemed perfect but as he sat there thinking of Annie he was so sad that she couldn't get beyond the fact that Pat and Molly had let them down. His musings were broken by Mrs Corr coming in rubbing her hands. She was finished for the day and he suddenly realised he had been sitting in her back room for several hours. Would you like a fresh mug of tea she asked as she took out some scones from a tin in the press, I have to do up the books before I go home and I always like a mug of tea first. Paddy realised he was hungry and thirsty and he gratefully accepted the offer as he still had to make his way up to Father Murphy. Cora Corr knew everything that went on in the village, she was aware of Pat Quinn having gone to England and she knew what was in the telegram. She knew what was in every telegram that ever passed through the post office, she knew when a letter came from England or America, and she knew when they didn't, but she never opened her mouth to anyone or divulged anything that went on in her place of work. She was as silent as a priest in the confessional Paddy thought to himself as she sat down at the small table.

We have been having lovely weather she said to him as he munched on the delicious scone that she had drowned in butter and jam. He nodded and decided to take the bull by the horns as it were, You know Cora what was in that telegram and I have no idea what to do, Annie has taken to the bed and refused to have anything to do with the whole business. Cora looked at him shrewdly, well If it was me in that situation and I had a son and a grandson coming to live with me I'd be singing it from the rooftops and I wouldn't care what anyone thought. Paddy looked at her and felt terrible as he realised that herself and her husband Mick had been married as long as himself and Annie and had no children at all. If it was left to me he said I would too. I was on my way to Father Murphy to see if he would intervene when you caught me. Cora looked at him, well if you want my advice and I rarely give it, I think you are right about Father Murphy's intervention but I also think you should go over to Mc Gee's tomorrow and meet your grandchild. Eoin Mc Gee obviously has no such hang ups about the situation and he is one of our most respected citizens. Annie will come round eventually, wait and see.

Father Murphy's housekeeper let him in to the presbytery, sit down Paddy I'll get his Reverence for you she was dying to know what he wanted and as discreet as Mrs Corr was, the priest's housekeeper would eat news out of a bucket as Annie was fond of saying. Well Paddy what ails you said Father Murphy coming into the parlour, bring us in some tea he said turning to the housekeeper. Paddy intervened quickly, no thanks Father he said I just want a word. The priest sat down and motioned Paddy to do the same, Paddy looked at the housekeeper who was still hovering in the doorway Father Murphy caught the nervousness of the look his Parishioner threw at the door. That will be all he said to the woman who was standing in the doorway, close the door on your way out and I Won't be needing anything else this evening.

The Priest went over to the glass cabinet that was arranged along the wall beside the fireplace, he took out two glasses and poured a generous amount of brandy into each of them, you look like you might need some help he said as he sat down once more. Paddy wasn't used to drinking at all and he took a big gulp out of the glass and nearly choked himself as the fiery liquid went down his gullet, The tears came out of his eyes as Father Murphy said easy now Paddy take your time, it can't be as bad as all that. The brandy seemed to give him courage and he told the whole story to the priest who listened without interruption. Now, Annie has taken this news shocking bad and has taken to the bed. You are the only one that I think she will listen to. Father Murphy was silent for a long time as Paddy pulled himself together. Well he said at last it is not an ideal situation but it is not the first and Won't be the last time that this has happened. Is Pat sure the child is his. Well yes Father Paddy said awkwardly he says it happened before Molly and my daughter Mary went to England and got caught in the war over there. Father Murphy remembered well, he also remembered that he thought Pat Quinn was a bit of a ladies man at that time and as far as he could remember Molly Mc Gee was only a child of seventeen or eighteen. He did his best at the Parish dances but he couldn't go home with everyone as they left the dance hall. Times had changed since then and the young people seemed to have less respect for his collar. Well he mused to himself at least they are married and the child will have a name and two parents and he will have grandparents. It would be the talk of the place for a while but no doubt would be forgotten before long. He said as much to Paddy and promised to go down to talk to Annie the next day. Paddy heaved a sigh of relief as he thanked the priest and gave him five pounds. He was feeling a bit heavy headed after the brandy and decided to go for a walk around the lake to clear his head. Father Murphy had no such problem and went back into the parlour and poured himself another little drop.

Annie Quinn was sitting up in the bed looking at Paddy as if she could kill him. He had just told her that the Parish Priest was coming to talk to her as he was sick of the way she was behaving. He had never spoken to her in that tone in all the years that they had been married. He usually took the easy option and kept out of her way when any ruckus took place. She was just as shocked that Paddy was standing up to her as to the fact that the priest was coming and the house was upside down, she almost knocked her husband over in her rush to get out of bed and get dressed. She was so upset that she didn't even continue with the giving out. She was surprised to see the kitchen was still intact when she finally arrived downstairs, Paddy was sitting at the table eating a boiled egg and she saw that he has set a place for her with another boiled egg sitting in its cup. She sat down and looked at him from under her eyebrows as he munched away. What time is his reverence coming she asked in a quieter tone of voice, as she realised she was now going to have to face the situation whether she liked it or not. He didn't say, replied Paddy still not looking at her, but I do know what time The Doctor and our grandson are coming at, they will be arriving around three pm. They are not coming here but going straight to Mc Gee's house where we are invited over at anytime after that. He also informed her that Pat and Molly would arrive on Saturday and would also be staying at Mc Gees. They will be living there in fact, he stated as the house is now Molly's. Annie was struck dumb, firstly she didn't want Molly coming into her house and now that she knew she wasn't she suddenly contrarily wanted her to come. It dawned on her an instant afterwards, that Pat wouldn't be living at home anymore either. Her world was falling apart. She looked so woebegone that Paddy felt sorry for her. He got up and put his hand on her shoulder, Talk to Father Murphy and listen to what he has to say. I am going out on the farm now but I will be back in lots of time to get ready go over to Mc Gees. I would dearly love for you to come too, but you have to want to come and you have to be very welcoming if you don't want to lose your son as well as your grandson and daughter-in-law he said as he went out the door.

Annie sat at the table for a long time and thought back to the time herself and Paddy were the new bride and groom coming into the house, Paddy's mother and father were both alive at that time and they couldn't have been more welcoming. Her mother -in-law had been great when Meg and Dan were babies, they never had a cross word, she had passed on before Pat and Mary were born. Her father -in-law had died just a few months before his wife and she didn't seem to have the will to live after he was gone. Annie felt ashamed of herself and realised how lucky she was that Pat was still going to be around. She got up to tidy up the parlour and light the fire before Father Murphy came, when she heard someone coming in the back door. I ll be out in a minute she shouted as she put a match to the turf that Paddy had set up in the grate, she almost fell into the half lit fire as Father Murphy shouted back, there's no hurry. Annie got up off her knees and rushed into the kitchen where to her shame father Murphy was sitting down at the kitchen table that was still littered with the remains of the boiled egg breakfast. I' m so sorry Father she spoke rapidly as her heart seemed to be somewhere up in her neck pounding away at a mile a minute. Take your time Annie he said as she threw dishes, eggshells and tea leaves into the sink with a wild abandon that was most unlike the usual sedate matron that always presented herself to the priest. Sit down woman he shouted before she threw the teapot that was now in her hand in on top of everything else that was in the sink. We need to talk. Annie sat down like a stone. Father Murphy was not the ogre that he pretended to be and he knew that the heart was scalded in the woman in front of him. Look Annie what has happened is not right, but it can't be undone, Pat did the right thing by Molly as soon as he knew of her predicament. They are married and are coming back to live in the Parish along with their son, now I would rather if it passed off as smoothly as possible. Annie suddenly broke in how will that happen the child is ten years old, Maybe he is not even Pat's she whispered. Annie, Father Murphy continued, Pat and Molly are

204

good people and if Molly Mc Gee says the child is Pats then he is. I will meet you all outside the Church on Sunday and we will chat as if the child was only born yesterday and as if his parents were married nine months before that Now for God's sake will you put on the kettle and give me a cup of tea.

Paddy met the priest on the lane way up to the farmhouse, he tipped his cap and said thank you Father, I hope all is well. All is Fine Paddy God Bless you and I will see you at Mass on Sunday. Paddy went into the back kitchen to wash his hands before he changed into his good shirt and jacket. He was stunned to see Annie in her best suit sitting at the table staring into space. I'm ready whenever you are she said as Paddy just nodded and went to get ready.

They took the five minute walk to Mc Gees in silence and as Paddy rang the doorbell he could hear Annie taking a deep breath. Eoin Mc Gee answered the door immediately and ushered them into the front room. You' re very welcome he said please sit down, Patrick is upstairs, I told him to wait there until I call him. Please don't take this the wrong way he said, but my daughter's happiness is very important to me, as you know my wife hasn't been well for a long time and probably when Molly was younger we were both negligent in her care, I with my busy practice and as for Maud, well she never really settled here. I know how much time Molly spent at your house and how much she valued your friendship. I have no blame to put on Pat, we have had a very enlightening chat and I am proud to call him my son-in-law. I hope that you both will welcome my daughter into your family too. Annie hung her head in shame, she was thoroughly sick at how she had ranted and raved first at Mary and then at Pat. Paddy knew instinctively how she was feeling and taking her hand he said we will be delighted to welcome Molly into the Quinn family, I believe they are going to be living here Paddy said giving Annie time to recover her composure. Eoin nodded it seems to be what they want and it will be convenient for Pat to work at the farm. Molly has plans to open up the surgery and help out as a nurse/midwife in the district. This was news to the Quinns who listened as The Doctor proudly told them how Molly had studied and passed all of her nursing exams while still caring for Patrick. Annie grew more and more ashamed as she realised how her well her new daughter -in-law had done under the circumstances. Eoin Mc Gee stood up, I think it's time you met your grandson he said as he went to the bottom of the stairs and called out to Patrick. Annie was the nearest to the door as he came in his Auburn hair glinting and his green eyes looking at them for approval. He already loved his Grandpa Mc Gee and hoped that he would like these other grandparents as well. The woman who was his granny Quinn gasped as she saw Pat's double walk towards her and before Paddy got a chance to stand up she had him in her arms, the tears streaming down her face as she realised what she could have lost. Oh my darling boy was all she could gasp as Patrick suffered the stranglehold she had on him, Paddy laughed will you stop trying to choke him, its my turn for a hug now, Annie reluctantly let go of the boy that she had tried to pretend wasn't her grandchild and let him go to Paddy. Patrick hadn't spoken yet and as he hugged his Grandpa Quinn as he now called him they were amazed at his English accent so like Kate's when she had arrived over a year ago. The boy was overwhelmed with all the love that was coming his way, from having had just his mother in his life he now had all these lovely people and as well as that Auntie Mary, Uncle George and Kate were coming down here on Saturday when his mum and dad would be arriving from England. His dad was going to show him all the places that he had played in when he was a boy, he was going to teach him how to catch a fish and how to play Irish football which was quite different to Rugby. He was going to be starting at his dad's old school and later on in the week he was going to meet two boys called Jamie and Joe Collins who would take him there. Their father was a friend of his dad.

Mary packed the clothes that they needed for the weekend at the farmhouse, she wasn't looking forward to staying with her mother and would have made an excuse not to go only Pat had begged her to and of course she was dying to see Molly and Patrick again. Kate was so excited to be seeing her cousin also she had so much to tell him. George came in as she was zipping up their case. You had better tell me now he said looking at her with a puzzled expression what I can say or can't say or I am bound to put my foot in it, I never know with your mother if she is serious about some of the mad things that she comes out with, Oh she is

serious all right said Mary with a frown. She is furious
that we knew about Molly and Patrick and that she was
the last to know. I don't understand said George, when
she did get to know she blew her top, Do you think she
will stop Molly from going in to the house. Well it
depends on who's watching if Doctor Mc Gee is there
she Won't let on to be mad she 'll act all holy and pious
but I don't fancy being in Molly's shoes when she gets
her on her own. I 'll try and act as a buffer until I see
Molly on her own myself. Maybe she 'll be softened
when she sees Patrick and how much he resembles Pat.
She loves Kate and maybe she will love Patrick too Mary
said doubtfully as George took the case out to the car.
They were getting a telephone installed next week and
Mary would be able to ring Molly at the post office or
maybe the surgery if Molly could call over there. It
would be great to meet up again. Mary missed her
friend and she was sure that Molly had missed her too.

Chapter Twenty

The bride and groom were due to arrive in the afternoon and the Hills planned to be there before them, it would be a tight squeeze with everyone staying on Saturday night but they would have to make the most of it. Pat and Molly would probably be in Pats old room and there was a press bed in the parlour where Patrick could sleep, Mary George and Kate always slept in Mary's old bedroom which would probably be turned into Patrick's room when they got settled. They pulled up just before lunch time and Kate was out of the car like a shot, she ran in through the back door as Mary and George struggled with their belongings. Mary was composing herself to talk nicely to her mother even though they hadn't parted on the best of terms on the last weekend that they were down. She was puzzled as to why her mother hadn't come out to greet them like she usually did, oh God she thought is she still in a sulk when out the back door came Annie with Kate on one arm and Patrick on the other. Mary stood with her mouth open while George dropped the case with what sounded very much like "Bloody Hell" Now George no swearing in front of my grandchildren please Said Annie as if this was the most normal thing in the world and the sky didn't fall.

Mary ran to Patrick who gently disentangled himself from Annie with a polite, excuse me granny please and he ran towards his Aunt who said are you here all ready, we thought we'd be here before you, where are your mum and dad, Patrick beamed up at her. They haven't arrived yet, I came over with granddad Mc Gee on Thursday and we have been staying at his house at night but I have been here at the farm with granny and granddad Quinn every day, haven't I granny he said putting out his hand to her. Indeed you have my dote said Annie taking his arm as if she had been saying it all his life. Kate was feeling a bit left out at this stage and commandeered Patrick to take her up to Granddad Paddy who was still up in the meadow. The children ran off with much laughter and an admonishment from Annie to tell Paddy that lunch was ready. George looked at Mary to see what he was supposed to do next but she shook her head as she hadn't a clue how this miracle had taken place. Come on in said Annie you must be famished, I have the meal on the table, I have it set in the kitchen as I don't want to mess up the parlour as its ready for Pat and Molly. Mary digested this piece of information with a grin, they were not ''the visitors '' any more, they were going to eat in the kitchen which was much cosier than the parlour ever was. I Won't make the tea until Paddy comes in would you like to go after the children George and walk back with them. George looked at Mary to see if this was what he should do and she nodded at him so off he went. Annie had her back to Mary as she said, I am so sorry for the way I behaved the last weekend that you were here, I am ashamed of all the hurtful things that I said. I will try and make it up to Pat and Molly when they come. I love that boy already he is so lovely and polite and he is the image of Pat. I wish they were going to be living here,

Mary looked at her in surprise, what do you mean mam she said, they are going to live in Molly's old home Annie replied, Doctor Mc Gee has given it over to them and Molly is hoping to use the surgery, she is a fully qualified nurse and midwife you know. Is she indeed smiled Mary who had gone through the all of the awful weeks of studying and suffering of the midwifery exams with Molly. That is wonderful news, and Pat will be near enough and sure you'll see them every day. Don't worry about the things you did and said in the past, it's the future that matters.

Eoin Mc Gee had gone to the Station to pick up the newly married couple, they were all going back to Quinns for the celebration dinner. Annie had two roast chickens a gammon of ham, together with a big pot of potatoes, Carrot, parsnips and cabbage fresh from the garden. She had made jelly and custard the night before with the help of Patrick who had often helped the nuns in the kitchen when his mum was busy. Annie was amazed at how good he was at cleaning the potatoes and vegetables, he also knew how to set the table beautifully as he was used to doing that job for Sister Monica. Annie was bursting with pride as she tried to forget the horror she had felt on hearing of his existence. Sure tis a treasure you are she had said to Patrick when all was ready.

They were all sitting chatting in the kitchen when the car pulled into the yard, there was a mad scramble for the door as everybody tried to be first out. Kate was the most nimble and from her many games of football with

Lily and the Banaghan boys she was able to duck out under the legs of the adults, she tore over to her uncle Pat who was helping Molly out of the car, She was suddenly shy as she hadn't seen Molly for so long and she hung back at the last minute, but Pat swept her up in a hug and a laughing Molly looked at her, Oh Kate she said you have grown so much and she folded the little girl into her arms. Everybody got in on the act, Mary and George couldn't get over how well and happy Molly looked and as for Pat he was beaming from ear to ear. Annie Quinn was the only one who had held back somewhat, Paddy had shaken the hand of the bride and groom as he welcomed Molly home. Patrick was hugging his mum and his dad when Molly noticed Annie standing to one side, She went over to the older woman and put her hand on her arm, thank you for having us for dinner she said as Annie with a sob took her into her arms, Thank you for my grandson and for making that eejit Pat so happy. Pat who was looking on apprehensively sighed with relief, it would be all right. They all trooped in to partake of Annie's dinner.

They were standing outside the Church on Sunday after Mass as was the custom, Father Murphy stood shaking hands with his parishioners as they left the Church and spoke of the lovely weather they were having '' an Indian Summer'' I think they call it he said, as the entire Quinn family flanked by Jim and Kitty Collins with their two boys, Doctor Mc Gee and Cora and Mick Corr stood in the Sunday Sunshine. People shook hands and wished the bride and groom the very best and if they thought the boy along with them was the image of Pat Quinn nobody said so. Annie stood beside Paddy holding the hand of Patrick, and to all and sundry she announced proudly this is my Grandson and the sky didn't fall.

Mary was going over to Sheehan's shop. Tom had made the decision to sell to P.C. Daws Ltd., and George and himself had come to a very amicable sale price, however as the firm didn't want any of the dry goods on the property and they wanted it emptied by the end of the month Tom and Sally decided to have a "sale". They had put up posters in the window, EVERYTHING GOING FOR HALF PRICE AT SALE ON TUESDAY EVERYTHING MUST GO. The interest and excitement in the village was phenomenal, Tom and Sally had found stuff that they had forgotten they even had, Mary and George had spent an entire day along with them pricing and putting things on display. Mary was going to help out on the day of the sale The Twins, Terry and Kate were going over to stay with Lizzie Banaghan, Baby Christy was being minded by a reluctant Angela over at their new home. Tim Carey would help out with the baby if help was needed.

The day of the sale dawned bright and clear on a crisp October morning, Tom was surprised as he opened the rickety shutters for the last time to see a growing crowd of people all straining to get in, He shouted out to Sally and Mary who were having a cup of tea in the back to get ready, there seems to be a lot of people out there he threw over his shoulder as he pulled back the bolt. Ballybrae had never seen anything like it.Sally thought to herself that everyone had gone a bit mad, they were fighting over old tins of custard, tins of peaches, packets of Peas, tins of shoe polish, shoe laces, and the bags of sugar and tea had been gone in a shot. What is wrong with people she whispered to Mary, they all love a bargain Mary whispered back as she placed ten pairs of shoe laces into a bag for Miss Conlon, Kate's teacher. Tom was in charge of the till as the women wrapped and bagged and he had to go into the back room twice to empty the money in to the safe. They were all beginning to flag around 2 o'clock and the stock was starting to diminish when Rose and Terence Sheehan arrived. Rose had a big basket of sandwiches and an apple tart, go on into the back and get this into you she said to Tom, your father and I can manage the place for a half an hour and bring those two hard working women with you. They needed no second bidding and headed in to put on the kettle. At seven O' clock the last item a packet of custard cream biscuits that had slipped down behind the counter was all that was left in the once packed shop. Tom momentarily had a pang of regret but it didn't last as he thought of the freedom they all would have. No more early morning papers, no more late nights at the beck and call of anyone who might have forgotten to get the bread. He heaved a sigh of relief as he locked the door for the last time.

Mary was tired but glad that she was able to help her friends out in the "sale of the century" as George had jokingly been calling it, she was heading over to Banaghans to collect Kate and had brought the packet of custard creams for the children, she also had a basket of tea, sugar and flour for Lizzie as she hadn't the chance to avail of the half-price sale. There was no sign of anyone around Banaghans but she could hear children's laughter coming from over at Larry Devine's farm yard, she left her precious basket at the kitchen door and headed over to Devine's. She blinked in surprise as she saw Lizzie above on Larry 's tractor with Larry behind her, his arms around her showing her how to hold her hands on the steering wheel, the children were all dancing around the tractor shouting at Lizzie to put her foot down, while Lizzie her hair hanging into her eyes was holding onto the steering wheel like a life line. Well look at you Mary said as she came upon the unsuspecting Lizzie, You 'll be getting a tractor next, Lizzie up ended Larry almost knocking him to the ground as she quickly disentangled herself from his arms and scrambled down red faced from the machine. Don't mind me said Mary laughing at the two red faced adults and shrieking children. I have Custard creams over at the house for you she said to the children who immediately tore off in the direction of Banaghan's. By the way she said George got four complimentary tickets to the cinema in Carrickmore as he took an ad out in their trailer section, Would the two of you like to come with us it's next Wednesday night. There is a great film showing that was made in Ireland starring Maureen O' Hara and John Wayne, it's called "The Quiet Man" Larry looked as if he was going to refuse when Lizzie said I can't leave the children, there is no need to worry about them Mary said I have Angela Sheehan minding Kate and she can mind Lily as well, The boys will be fine with Sally and Tom over at their new home, I have already asked them so you have no excuse, Lizzie gave up and said primly that would be lovely, Larry wasn't sure if she meant for herself to go or if she was including him in her ''that would be lovely'' Mary gave him no choice as she said that's great we will collect you both at seven thirty on Wednesday. As the two women followed the children back to Banaghan's Lizzie turned on Mary how could you put me in that awkward position, I don't think Larry wanted to go. Don't be daft said Mary grinning he doesn't know what he wants yet. You will take the sight out of his eyes on Wednesday night and he won't know what hit him. Lizzie was still grumbling away as they came upon the empty wrapping paper from the custard creams blowing in the breeze.

Chapter Twenty One

Wednesday night came and all-day long Larry had pondered about what a man wore to the cinema, he only had one good suit and he would feel like a proper eejit dolled up in that for going to see a film, sure it was dark in there anyway. Eventually he wore his good black trousers a white shirt and his red tie with the black spots on it. He had a newish black Cardigan and he decided to carry it in case it was chilly at the cinema. He rarely looked in the mirror except to shave and was totally unaware of how handsome he looked. Lizzie was also wondering all day what she should wear for the outing. She hadn't been to the cinema since she took Seamus and Sean to see a cowboy film some years ago, Sean woke up several times in the night afterwards shouting the Indians are coming and the sweat pouring off him. That was the end of the pictures for them. She was looking at her choice of dresses, the blue one that Mary had given her, a red gingham one that was as old as the hills and a black pleated skirt. She was looking for a blouse to go with the skirt when Mary arrived with a box of clothes that she threw on the kitchen table, Please take these off my hands she said sitting down with her hand on her back, she was beginning to look quite big now and was longing for Christmas to be over and the new baby to be in it's pram. I think this baby is a trained footballer she laughed. It is scoring goals at this very minute. Lizzie was sympathetic as she put the kettle on for the tea, I can't be taking any more clothes from you she said you have given me enough already, Mary waved her protestations away, You are doing me a favour, I Won't be getting into any of this stuff again and it will save me from having to find place for them. They went through the skirts, dresses, cardigans and blouses. Lizzie was enchanted it was like birthdays and Christmas all at once. The stuff seemed to her to be brand new and she put her arms around Mary to thank her, I don't need any thanks Mary replied as she took the cup of tea from Lizzie, Lets pick out something for you to wear tonight. They decided on a yellow dress with daisies around the neck and hem and a white cardigan to go with it. You will knock Larry sideways Mary said jokingly. Lizzie was immediately on the defensive, I 'm not getting dressed up for him, I am getting dressed up for myself. Of course you are said Mary wisely finishing her tea and getting up to go. We will see you at seven thirty and then we will pick up Larry. I am really looking forward to the film I love John Wayne and Maureen O' Hara.

Lizzie was ready at six O' Clock, she couldn't get over how quiet the house was without any of the children getting in her way and she had decided to get ready as soon as they were gone. She took her time brushing her long wavy hair, she gave it the hundred brushes that her long dead mother had told her always made the hair shine, and as she looked at it falling in waves around her shoulders she realised how right her mother was, it shone like a chestnut. She wondered what her mother would think of her dolling herself up to go out and what Denis would have said and then she seemed to hear

Madame Zelda's hoarse voice "Your destiny awaits you do not miss it " she knew in her heart that Denis would want her to be happy as she looked at herself in the mirror. A knock on the door startled her out of her musings, who on earth can that be she thought, what am I going to do, It might be Father Hoey was the next mad thought that came into her head and she rushed to get an apron to throw on over her finery as she took two clips from the shelf and clipped back her hair, How am I going to get rid of whoever it is before Seven Thirty. She opened the door to find Larry standing there looking as handsome as John Wayne himself, he was holding a bunch of late Summer Roses in his hand which he thrust at her as if they were stinging him. Lizzies mouth fell open in shock as they stood looking at each other. I didn't want George to have to be stopping twice so I decided to come over, is that all right he said as lizzie still stood like a statue with the roses in her hand. Even Denis had never given her flowers. I saw it in the films Larry said pointing to the flowers. Thank you whispered Lizzie, I have never had flowers given to me before. She went off to get a vase to put them in. Larry sat down at the kitchen table and felt quite pleased with himself for having being the first one to give her flowers he would have been even more pleased if he could have seen Lizzie in the back kitchen pulling the clips out of her hair with abandon and flinging the apron into the turf box.

The film was wonderful, Maureen O' Hara was so beautiful and played the part of Mary Kate Danagher so well, Lizzie's heart was in her mouth as she thought

Mary Kate's thick lump of a brother wasn't going to let her marry the handsome John Wayne who played Sean Thornton. She squirmed and put her hands on her eyes when the fight took place in the meadow, She hardly noticed when Larry put his arm around her when she squealed.she put her head on his shoulder and kept her eyes closed as she whispered to him, is the fight over, indeed it is said Larry you can look now, they are going back home together. But he kept his arm around her for the rest of the film and she never moved an inch.

That night after the film George went to stop at Devines to drop off Larry but Mary gave him a pinch and whispered keep going to Banaghan's which he did with much muttering and changing of gears. Neither Lizzie or Larry tried to stop him, will you come in for a cup of tea before the boys come home Lizzie asked as she made to get out of the car. That would be nice said George, no it wouldn't said Mary giving him another pinch we don't need any tea, go ahead in and have your tea and we will collect the boys and bring them back here. Lily was staying overnight in Hills as a special treat. Larry walked with Lizzie up to the front door, he wasn't sure if he should go in or go home, but Lizzie kept walking so he followed her in. Sit down while I put on the kettle we will have a cup drank before the boys come in, Larry didn't sit down instead he paced up and down the flagged kitchen floor. He wasn't sure of himself but the pleasant reception of the Roses had given him a bit of hope, Would you like to come to the cinema with me some night on our own he asked not looking at Lizzie but at the floor as if he was counting the flagstones.

Lizzie smiled at him, that would be lovely, sit down there now before you wear the floor out and we will pick a night but no cowboy films please. Larry laughed, there wasn't really a great choice but he didn't care as long as they had an arrangement. They sat comfortably in each others company until the boys burst in the door, if they were surprised to see Larry there they didn't show it. Seamus immediately started a conversation about tractors and machinery while Sean as usual looked for something to eat and he asked Larry to get it for him. Lizzie gave him a clip on the ear dont be annoying the man she said, Sean looked surprised, sure I'm hungry, Larry is the nearest one to the bread, Lizzie was heartened to see how well her boys got on with Larry. It was the start of the courtship that would probably garner a good bit of talk but Neither of them were gossipmongers so it wouldn't bother them.

Mary was heaving herself up out of the armchair she was now the full of it and had to prise herself out. They were going to Pat and Molly's for Christmas dinner and for the first time in her married life Annie Quinn was not in charge of the turkey, herself and Paddy were also going over to Mc Gees as she still called it. Eoin Mc Gee was arriving from Dublin after he had been to Mass and he was picking up his wife Maud and bringing her out the of Nursing home for the day. Patrick was in a fluster of excitement, this would be his first Christmas with all four of his grand parents. George was bringing over the box camera and he was going to take a picture of them all for posterity. The smell of cooking coming out from the kitchen was a mixture of roast turkey, ham, stuffing and Christmas pudding. Molly had been well grounded in the Kitchen of St. Bernard's and Annie couldn't fault a single thing. Patrick had set the table and was most particular about the napkins, the place settings, and the crackers. He had made little name tags for each place and decorated them with holly. The whole place was tinged with an air of excitement. Molly was a bit sad that her mother probably wouldn't know where she was but at least they all knew she was there along with them for the festivities. The Christmas tree was in the parlour and had loads of presents underneath. They were going to open them after dinner. Patrick and Kate were like mad things, they couldn't wait for the present opening and Molly had to give them jobs to keep them quiet. Doctor McGee arrived with Maud and as he carefully helped her out of the car he saw her looking around in puzzlement. Where am I she said as he led her up the path to the house that he had brought her to when they were first married. She took in all of the strange people in the house and hung on to him for dear life. It's all right my dear he said putting her into an armchair beside the fire. She always felt the cold and he placed the cashmere shawl that he had brought for her tenderly around her shoulders. Maud relaxed somewhat as Molly came over to kneel on the floor beside her. You look well Mother she said quietly as she put her hand on her knee, Maud stroked Molly's hair and began to croon rock-a-by baby, The tears fell fast and furious from Molly's eyes as she sat there remembering her mother singing to her as a small child. Maud stopped as suddenly as she started and fell asleep in the heat of the fire. She'll be fine Eoin stated, we will give her some dinner when we are finished, she doesn't like a large crowd around her when she is eating. That dinner was delicious Molly, Paddy said as he sat back in his chair, indeed it was said Annie graciously as if she couldn't believe her daughter -in-law could have produced such a fine meal. Are you as full as a tick Grandad grinned Kate, I am indeed my pet he smiled, What is a tick asked Patrick seriously as Kate and her grandfather shared a secret smile. We will introduce you to one when the Summer comes and you are out in the meadow Paddy said, ruffling his grandson's Auburn curls. Pat stood up come on it's time to open these presents he shouted, he had gazed in pride at his wife and son all morning and he looked so happy that even Annie was forced to admit that her son was a new man, himself and George had gone to Carrickmore a few weeks back and bought Kate and Patrick two shiny new bicycles. They had been hidden in Quinn's barn and were now under a sheet in the scullery to be produced when all the other present giving was over. Everyone was delighted with their presents and amid much laughter and hugging, Pat said we have three more surprises. Everyone looked at him in surprise including George who was thinking of the two surprises out in the back kitchen, One is for you Patrick and one is for you Kate, the other one is for everybody, they all waited as Molly went to join her husband, there will be another Quinn please God at next year's Christmas party he announced proudly as the place erupted and Mary tried to get out of the chair but got stuck, Eoin and Paddy

223

reached them at the same time as George helped Mary up to hug them both, Kate and Patrick were still in the dark as to who this other person could be they had been sitting beside Annie whom, now to their astonishment was crying her eyes out, what's wrong granny Kate asked putting her arms around her, why are you crying, Annie wiped her tears on the sleeve of her good cardigan, I'm crying because I am so happy to be getting another grandchild, The children starting whooping with delight as the penny dropped and the second two surprises were forgotten in the melee that ensued. Annie went over to her daughter-in-law and put her arms around her much to the delight of Mary, Pat, Paddy and Eoin, Thank you for the best Christmas present anyone could get she said tearfully, I am so sorry for being so mean to everyone in the Summertime and I hope you will all forgive me. George felt enormous pity for his mother-in-law and even though he had been on the receiving end of her wrath several times, he knew her heart was in the right place, she was such a stickler for "the right thing" that he took the heat off her by asking what about the other surprises for Patrick and Kate.

Chapter Twenty Two

Mary was sitting in her kitchen with Sally and Lizzie, The children were out in the fields gathering rushes to make St. Bridget's crosses. I remember feeling like this just before Kate was born Mary said as she stroked her tummy, what way is that asked Sally as she put the kettle on, tea was always a great cure for everything. Sure, you only have three weeks to go, you Won't feel it flying by, I had a feeling as if the baby was trying to get out Mary said, anyway let's talk about something else, how is the big romance going Lizzie ? to their surprise Lizzie didn't go all defensive as she usually did, she just said fine, What do you mean fine demanded Sally, we want to know everything. They looked at her and she blushed, well actually, Larry is very romantic, the two women tried and failed to see the shy Larry in this light. He proposed to me the other night when we were out for a walk in the moonlight, he actually went down on one knee. This was too much for the two women who were waiting with bated breath, Mary tried to jump up as Sally pulled her out of the chair and they rushed over to Lizzie, Oh my God who would think it, We are so happy for you they both burst out, This is great news. Lizzie continued, I have told the children, of course All Seamus can think about is that he will be gaining a tractor, while Sean and Lily are very happy that they will be gaining a new daddy. Larry told them that he wasn't their real dad but that he would look after them and me as if he was. We are going to get married quietly at

Easter with just the children and you, my friends present. We have been to see Father Hoey who is going to perform the ceremony. Well aren't you the dark horse said Mary, all uncomfortable baby feelings forgotten in the excitement of Lizzie's news. They made all sorts of plans for the wedding day and Sally announced that if Lizzie would permit them, the Sheehan's would host the wedding breakfast. It would be chance to show off the new parlour /dining room that they had just finished decorating and furnishing and Mary not to be outdone announced I will make the wedding cake this baby will be out by then. Lizzie was delighted and thanked her friends as the back door burst open and Lily, Kate and Terry burst in with their arms full of fat green rushes.

Mary had been feeling very uncomfortable all evening and as George was out playing golf with his new best friend, Father Hoey, with whom he had been doing a round of the local Golf links in town one evening a week for the past while she didn't want to let Kate go over to Banaghan's. This did not go down well as Lily and Kate had a new project, walking up and down the aisle as they called it. Lizzie had asked them to be her bridesmaids at her wedding and they were beside themselves with excitement, Sean was going walk his mother up the Aisle and Seamus was to be Larry's best man. The girls were going to wear their communion dresses which with a little adjustment and additions had been altered by Mrs Canny to fit them. Larry insisted on getting the boys new suits. He was going to live in Banaghan's so as to give least upheaval to the children and he would work both farms with the help of Lizzie. Why can't I go over to play'' Aisles ''with Lily mammy Kate pleaded, they both started in shock as Mary let a shout, Kate looked at her mother with a white face as Mary moaned again, Its all right sweetheart, I think the baby might be coming I want you to be a good girl and go straight over to Terry's Mammy and ask her to come back with you and then you can go over to Lily. Kate ran as fast as her legs could carry her, she ran in Sheehan's back door as Sally was coming out with the washing to the clothes line. Mrs Sheehan please come quick, my mammy is having the baby, Sally dropped the wash basket and ran shouting out to Tom to keep an eye on Christy. They got back at the same time as George who was taking his golf clubs out of the car boot. Leave them there and get the midwife Sally yelled at him as he stood with his mouth open. Go on she yelled again, Kate you go on over to Banaghan's and stay there until your daddy collects you, Kate was reluctant to leave but Sally gave her a hug, go on you will have a new brother or sister by the time your daddy gets you and your mammy will be fine. George had by this time gone to collect nurse Storey and Kate ran off to tell Lily the great news. Mary was moaning away and had by this time got herself up to the bedroom, she was drenched in sweat and Sally got her a wet facecloth for her forehead. The pains were coming fast and thick and Mary gripped Sally hand in a vice like clench. I thought that Mam and Molly would be here, they were both coming down at the end of the month to help deliver this baby she moaned. Sally held her hand don't worry George is gone for Nurse

Storey, she is an excellent midwife and they will be here any minute now. They were indeed there in ten minutes and as Sally gave way to the competent midwife she took stock of George who was looking worse than Mary at that moment. Come on downstairs and I 'll make you a drink of tea with something strong in it to calm your nerves, then I 'll go back up in case I'm needed. George gratefully followed her downstairs and sat at the kitchen table. It was the fastest delivery in history with a nine pounds Michael Hill arriving into the world in a hurry. The midwife gently cleaned him and placed him in his mother's arms, and as Sally came back upstairs, she was amazed to hear a baby crying. She ran into the room and saw Mary cradling her baby she shouted congratulations and ran down stairs again to get George, He never got to drink the tea that she had made as she ran in to Congratulate him also, I don't know if you have a son or a daughter she laughed I forgot to ask. George rushed up to see Mary sitting up with the baby in her arms as if it was no bother and with a smile on her face she handed the baby to George, Meet your son Michael she said, They had decided on calling the baby Michael if it was a boy after George's father and Ann if it was a girl, after Annie Quinn. George was over the moon he took the now quiet baby and beamed with pride at his wife and son, I think he looks like you George with his very fair hair and his blue eyes Mary announced as she suddenly felt very tired, Nurse Storey had done all the necessary clean up and was about to leave, I will be over later tomorrow to see this young man and yourself she said but I shouldn't imagine you'll have any bother with him, sure he nearly ready for solid food and the size of him. They thanked her and George went off to bring her home. Sally came back up when George left and said she would wait on until he came back, How are you feeling she asked Mary as she fixed her pillows, Mary said she was remarkably well everything considered, it was actually a very easy birth compared to the first one, he was here before I knew it. You'll be having another one soon so said Sally dryly, Mary grimaced, no thanks I think two is just enough for me. I hope Kate will love her new brother and not be jealous. Sally laughed and told her about Angela when the twins were born and herself and Tom had to feed one every time they cried as they were so small. Angela was furious and she kept trying to give them to anyone who came into the shop, eventually she realised that they were there to stay and she reluctantly accepted them, but she never forgave them for disrupting her peace and never ceased to remind them that she was there first, she was much younger than Kate is now though, and I think Kate will be like a second mother to Michael. George picked up his daughter on the way back from the midwifes, telling Lizzie about his new son, Kate couldn't wait to get home to see her brother, she couldn't believe after all these years of being an only child she now had a brother. She ran into the house and took the stairs two at a time. Her mammy was sitting up in bed looking much happier than the last time she saw her when she had left her to get Mrs Sheehan. She ran to hug her and then she shyly looked into the cradle beside the bed. He was so small and perfect and she loved him there and then with a passion that was to last all of their lives. He was her little brother and she would never let anyone hurt him. Mary heaved a sigh of relief it was going to be all right.

Michael Hill was baptised on a Sunday morning in early March. The Spring Sun was weakly trying to get through the clouds as they scudded across the sky. Annie and Paddy Quinn together with their Grandson Patrick had arrived in the church early as Annie wanted to say a prayer of thanksgiving for her new grandson and the fact that he was going to be Baptised, as she still had the occasional doubt about "the protestant element" of his lineage, The Sheehan's were all there with Christy asleep in his push chair and Sally hoping that he would stay that way, at least until after the Christening. Lizzie Banaghan and Larry Devine together with the children were also there. Pat and Molly Quinn who were to be Godparents were up at the Font together with Father Hoey. George's parents had decided against travelling at this time of year but were going to come over for a week later in the Summer. Mary George, Kate and the baby arrived with Mary whispering to Father Hoey and apologising for being late as the baby had been hungry and had to be fed.

We are gathered here my Friends boomed the priest for these Baptisms this morning, Baptisms that will celebrate the entrance of two new souls into the Catholic Church, They all looked at each other and down the Aisle to see who the other baby was but the rest of the Church was empty. I will first Baptise Michael Hill

230

and ask the Godparents to swear to uphold the rites of the Catholic Church. He proceeded to wet the baby 's head with water and baptised him in the Name of the Father, son and Holy Ghost. The baby was very good and looked up at the priest with his big blue eyes as his Godmother held him tightly, Pat held the baptismal candle and thought to himself that the next Christening that they would all be at together would be his and Molly's second child. He felt so happy and Blessed as the priest declared Michael to be a fully-fledged member of the Catholic Church, he almost missed the Priest's next words as he day dreamed, and now we will have the Baptism of Michael's Father George Hill who is converting to day. Father Hoey's words had everyone looking at each other in astonishment. I would like my mother-in-law and father -in-law to sponsor me on this journey George said looking at them both. Annie couldn't see her way as the tears flowed and Paddy took her arm to stand proudly beside George. Mary was speechless, he must have been having instruction all the time she thought he was playing golf. George Hill was received into the Catholic Church on the same day as his son Michael. Afterwards they all came out into the Sunshine and trooped over to Sheehan's newly decorated house for breakfast and '' The Sky didn't Fall''.

Printed in Poland
by Amazon Fulfillment
Poland Sp. z o.o., Wrocław

61409459R00139